He stepped over the threshold and closed the door.

She motioned him forward and put her finger to her lips. "Gabe is over here." She led him to the sofa in the corner of the sitting area.

He knelt beside his son and brushed a lock of hair off Gabe's face. The act was so tender and loving. Gabe didn't stir.

Bridget couldn't imagine her father ever doing anything so affectionate. Her parents had never been cruel nor hit her, but they had high expectations. If she didn't want to be reproached or put aside, she had better do as she was told. No love or compassion, just expectations. It wasn't until she'd come to know the Lord that she had felt anything like love. She hadn't known what she had been missing.

This man loved his children deeply. And if he loved them, then maybe he could come to love her...

Mary Davis is an award-winning author of more than a dozen novels. She is a member of American Christian Fiction Writers and is active in two critique groups.

Mary lives in the Colorado Rocky Mountains with her husband of thirty years and three cats. She has three adult children and one grandchild. Her hobbies are quilting, porcelain doll making, sewing, crafts, crocheting and knitting. Please visit her website, marydavisbooks.com.

Books by Mary Davis

Love Inspired Heartsong Presents

Her Honorable Enemy
Romancing the Schoolteacher

MARY DAVIS

Romancing the Schoolteacher

HEARTSONG
PRESENTS

™ LOVE INSPIRED BOOKS

ISBN-13: 978-0-373-48772-1

Romancing the Schoolteacher

Copyright © 2015 by Mary Davis

www.Harlequin.com

Printed in U.S.A.

Do not lie. Do not deceive one another.
—*Leviticus* 19:11

Dedicated in loving memory to my son Josh.

Also to my mom, Zola, and sisters Kath & Deb,
who tramped around the San Juan Islands with me.
It was a blast!

Chapter 1

San Juan Island, Washington Territory, Spring 1887

Bridget Greene stood at the back of her classroom and looked out over her students, ranging from the first to the eighth grade. The younger ones worked quietly on their reading while the older children took examinations.

Troy Morrison caught her attention. At fourteen, he was her oldest and most promising student. Most boys his age had to quit school and go to work to help support their families, often in the lime mines. Today, Troy promised to be mischievous.

He gently lifted Olivia Bradshaw's blond ponytail, which hung over his desk. He moved it slowly toward his inkwell, trying not to disturb the girl.

Bridget strode up next to his desk.

Troy's hand froze, and he slowly swiveled his head toward her.

She gave him her sternest look.

He dropped the ponytail.

Olivia reached for her hair and pulled it over her shoulder. Then she turned toward Bridget and smiled.

Bridget whispered to her, "Go back to work."

The girl did.

Bridget grabbed Troy's examination paper and motioned for him to follow her.

He struggled to untangle his gangly body from his seat and tripped over his feet. He hadn't gotten used to his growing body. He'd gone from short and chubby to lanky and awkward, shooting up at least five inches in the past two months alone. And he was suddenly interested in girls.

She set Troy's examination on her desk and pointed to her chair. She didn't dare make him sit with the youngest children as she would normally do to shame a disobedient student into behaving. He would never be able to extricate himself from one of the smaller desks, even if he managed to wedge himself into one.

As it was, he bumped her desk and the chair before managing to get himself in the seat.

She whispered, "Dipping her hair in ink is not the way to get Olivia's attention."

He scowled. "I don't *want* her attention."

But Bridget knew he did. He just didn't realize it yet. Even at eleven, Olivia was a pretty girl and promised to turn many a gentleman's head in the future.

"Finish your exam."

He hadn't even started and had only fifteen minutes to go.

She wandered the room.

Periodically, she looked at the watch pinned to her lapel as the final two minutes ticked off. "Time. Please put down your pencils."

She collected the exams and dismissed her pupils. They hustled out in a clatter of boots on wood and excited voices. Troy brought up the rear.

She quickly flipped through the exams and found the one she was looking for. "Troy, would you come here?"

The boy lumbered up the aisle and stood in front of her desk. His legs were longer than his trousers, and his wrists hung four inches below his shirt cuffs.

She studied him for a moment. He didn't seem to mind. She held up his mathematics exam. "You didn't answer one question. What happened?"

One bony shoulder rose and fell.

"You didn't even try. You know this material."

He kept his face neutral. "It's just school. It don't matter."

That didn't sound like her prize pupil. A student who had borrowed every book of hers he could. Mathematics was easy for him.

"School does matter. You are a very bright young man. You could go to college."

He stared at her, working his jaw back and forth as though he had something tough to chew on.

"You don't have to stay in Roche Harbor. You don't have to work in the lime mines. You can do anything you want."

He continued to stare. "May I leave now?"

She couldn't understand his change in behavior. "Do you want to work in the mines the rest of your life?"

He shook his head. "Pa says I'd be a better bet for working the kilns." His eyes brimmed with tears.

She could see him struggling to contain his emotions. "Your father wants you to quit school and work the lime kilns?"

"Family needs the money."

That was such a tough place for a young man to be. Caught between what he wanted and what his family needed. "Do *you* want to work the kilns or in the mines the rest of your life?"

"Don't matter what I want."

"Yes, it does. What do *you* want?"

"As soon as Pa can get it worked out with Mr. Keen, I'll be hired on." He blinked. A tear raced down his cheek. He slapped it away. "I like learning."

But she knew if his family needed the money, this boy would be set in a job he would likely never be able to rise out of. "What if you completed your education after work?"

"After?"

"We can figure a place to meet. I'll give you books, and you can ask me for whatever assistance you need." He was bright enough to learn on his own.

His forced, neutral expression slipped away and his eyes brightened. "Really? You'd help me?"

"Of course. I'll even talk to your father to see if he'll let you stay in school."

"He won't."

"It can't hurt to try." She looked past the boy to a man and two children standing at the back of her classroom. New students. She handed Troy his test. "See how many of these problems you can complete before you have to leave." She walked down the aisle to the man.

His mouth broke into a congenial smile that did something funny to her insides. She took a deep breath and pushed the odd sensation aside. "I'm Miss Greene."

He tipped his head. "I'm Lindley Thompson. These are my children, Gabe and Dora."

Gabe looked to be about seven, but Dora didn't look old enough for school yet. Maybe four. "Pleased to meet you."

Gabe said, "Hullo."

Dora smiled around her thumb and leaned into her father's leg.

Mr. Thompson wore miner's clothes, but there was something amiss about the family. "I've come to work in the lime mines. Gabe will be starting class tomorrow."

"And what about Dora?"

"She's only four."

"Four and a half," Dora said, not removing her thumb.

Bridget gazed at the girl. "So, you get to stay home with your mother."

Dora shook her head.

Bridget looked up at Mr. Thompson, and there was the strange feeling again.

"Their mother passed a few years ago."

"I'm so sorry. I have another four-year-old who comes to school. They could sit together."

"Thank you for the offer, but I've hired someone to look after her."

How could a single miner afford to pay someone to care for his daughter? Maybe he didn't realize how little the miners made and how much living cost. "If you change your mind, she is welcome."

She walked the man and his children out. The air filled with the screeches of dozens of seagulls circling near and far.

As they strode away, she realized what was out of place with them. Though they wore the clothes of a miner's family and were adequately dirtied, they weren't naturally dirty.

The smudges on the children's faces looked as though they were put there, not as if they got there from playing. And their clothes, as well. She had seen enough dirty children to know the difference.

Why was this man trying to make himself and his children look worn? A real miner would flaunt new clothes and make his children keep them clean, not purposely dirty them.

So if he wasn't a real miner, who was he?

Or maybe his circumstances had recently been reduced, and he didn't want the other miners to think him full of himself. Or that he thought he was better than them. Those

who worked the mines and the kilns banded together in a tight community.

As she walked back inside, Troy stood from her desk. She met him halfway down the aisle. "Do you need to leave?"

"Naw. I'm done."

He couldn't be.

He kicked a desk leg getting around her and then hit his shoulder on the doorway on his way out. Bridget cringed, but Troy kept going except for a sidestep adjustment.

The poor boy needed to learn where his new body stopped and started before he injured himself. Or something worse while working for the lime company.

She went to her desk and picked up his examination. Sure enough, every problem was answered. And at the bottom of the page, he had written, *I got them all right.*

She would see about that. How could he when he'd done the equations so quickly? She sat and pulled a sheaf of papers from her desk drawer, fingering through them for the right answer key. She checked his answers against hers and then sat back with a sigh. Indeed, he had answered them all correctly. She had to find some way to keep this boy in school.

Later that evening, Lindley finished cooking the simple meal of scrambled eggs and slightly burned pancakes for supper. His children didn't seem to mind. Or at least, neither of them said anything about his cooking ability. He couldn't prepare much, but his children never went hungry. They sat, bowed their heads, and he thanked the good Lord for the food.

"I want to go to school," Dora announced after the blessing.

"You can't," Gabe shot back.

"But I want to go. Please, Papa."

Lindley smiled at her, liking her enthusiasm. "I'm sorry. You're too young yet. School is for older children."

"But I *am* older."

He ruffled Dora's blond hair. "Yes, you are. But not quite old enough."

Dora tilted her head. "Teacher said."

Images of chestnut hair and eyes the color of the forest flitted through his mind. And the smile she had bestowed upon him and his children. Something had happened to him in that moment, but he couldn't determine what. The last thing he needed right now was to be thinking about the schoolteacher. He had a job to do and needed to devote his attention to that.

"Papa. Teacher said."

He focused back on his daughter. "I know, but Miss Greene has a lot of pupils to teach. Besides, Mrs. Weston is going to look after you. Now, eat your supper before it gets cold."

His daughter made a pouty face before digging into her pancakes.

Dora appeared to forget all about school for the rest of the evening. For that, he was grateful, and it allowed him to think of things other than the pretty schoolteacher.

Being on their own was going to be good for all three of them. Just him, Gabe and Dora without one sister or another trying to abscond with his children to make life easier for him. Their help only served to make him feel empty and abandoned. His family needed to realize he had the ability to keep Gabe and Dora fed and well cared for without interference. Though his family meant well, they made him feel incompetent as a parent. He needed to prove to them, as well as himself, he *was* capable.

He glanced around the pocket-size dwelling. It couldn't

be more than fifteen feet square. His bed on one side of the room and a second on the opposite wall, with a small cooking stove and a square eating table down the middle. If his sisters or even his parents saw this hovel, they would be here in a snap to rescue Gabe and Dora. But they were *his* children, and *he* would see to their well-being.

He dressed them for bed, and they climbed under the quilts of their shared bed, a straw mattress on the floor. Gabe's head at one end and Dora's poking out from the other.

Dora snuggled down and flopped her arms on top of the covers. "Tell us a story, Papa."

Gabe nodded.

"Once upon a time, there were two curious bunnies, a brother bunny and a sister bunny."

"A princess, Papa, a princess."

"And a dragon," Gabe said.

Lindley looked from his son to his daughter. "Once upon a time, there was a princess."

"Was she beautiful, Papa?"

"Of course. She had chestnut hair and eyes the color of the forest." He pictured the schoolteacher. Oops. Oh, well. He was sure his children wouldn't make the connection. "She was walking along when she came to an enchanted garden. Low hedgerows separated the different varieties of flowers—pinks, yellows, blues, purples, reds, oranges, whites and clear. But these were not like any flowers she'd seen before. The flowers were made of glass. She didn't know this garden was guarded by an army of dragonflies. So when she picked a pink-and-purple bloom, a swarm of dragonflies swooped in and carried her off to a cave where a big dragon lived."

By the time Lindley finished his tale, Dora's eyes were

closed, and Gabe's eyelids were drooping. He kissed them each on the forehead and headed for his own bed.

So much for not thinking of the schoolteacher. But what was the harm?

Chapter 2

The next morning, Bridget rang the school bell, and her students crowded into the classroom. She loved the children. Her first year teaching in Roche Harbor, she had thought she was blessed with an exceptional class of students who all wanted to learn.

She soon discovered that many of the older children would rather be in school than working in the mines. Their mind-set transferred down to the younger ones. She didn't care why her students were eager. She loved filling their minds with as much knowledge as possible for as long as they were in her charge. It broke her heart when good students were taken out of school to go to work. It just wasn't fair.

Her new pupil, Gabe Thompson, stood at the back of the room, waiting for a place to sit. What kind of student would he be?

Bridget put her hand on his small shoulder and guided him up the aisle to the front of the room. "Class, quiet down." When all the students had taken their seats and given her their attention, she spoke. "Class, this is Gabe."

"Hi, Gabe," the class said in unison.

"I expect you all to make him feel welcome. Daniel, please stand up."

The boy did. He was also seven. She hoped the boys

could forge a friendship. "Gabe will sit next to you. I expect you to help him out until he gets his bearings."

Gabe took his seat next to Daniel. He was quite attentive in the first morning section, taking his turn reading aloud and answering questions. A bright boy for his age. She would need to test him to determine his math and reading levels as well as his potential.

After an hour and a half, she released the children to play outdoors. The sun shone brightly on this crisp spring day.

She pulled her shawl closer as she watched her students frolicking in the school yard. The exercise was good for their learning process. She liked watching them interact with one another and took particular interest in those who sat alone. Today there were none.

The younger boys looked up to Troy and gathered around him. He liked the attention but kept casting glances toward Olivia.

Bridget hated to stop the fun, but she rang the handbell for the students to return to the classroom. They filed in, and she brought up the tail end. She strode up the aisle as her pupils settled into their seats. All twenty-two of them, including *two* four-year-olds. She crouched in front of the pair of girls. Aggie wiggled in her seat.

The other girl smiled up at her. "I'm in school."

"I see that. Your name is Dora, isn't it?"

The girl nodded eagerly.

"I thought your father had someone looking after you."

Dora shrugged. "She couldn't watch me. I came to school. You said I could."

She had obviously arrived during recess.

Gabe appeared next to them. "You aren't s'posed to be here."

Dora stiffened her shoulders. "Am too. Teacher said I could."

Bridget supposed it would be all right, if the woman couldn't watch the girl. A child her age couldn't very well be at home alone. "It's all right, Gabe. She can stay." Bridget turned back to Dora. She couldn't just send her away on her own. "You have to sit still and be quiet so the other students can learn, too."

Dora nodded eagerly.

Lindley pumped the bellows that fanned the fire in the lime kiln. Even though the day was cool, sweat ran down his face and soaked his clothes. If they didn't have the kiln hot enough, they couldn't change the limestone into quicklime and then hydrate it into slaked lime for masonry work. He was in the learning stages of the job, but he'd read up on the process of lime mining, so he knew a bit of what to expect and how things should be done. Gary Bennett, the man who was instructing him, gave him occasional nods of approval.

A commotion in the yard caught everyone's attention. Some hysterical woman.

Then the foreman called, "Thompson, get over here."

Lindley handed over the bellows arm to Mr. Bennett and trotted to the foreman. His breath caught in his throat, and he stopped short. "Mrs. Weston, what are you doing here? Is Dora all right?"

The heavyset woman had dried tears on her cheeks. "She's gone." She took in a shuddered breath. "I took my eyes off her for two seconds. I've looked everywhere. She isn't anywhere to be found."

Dora? Not his little girl. He should have left his children with his parents or older sister, Rachel, when they'd offered. But he had insisted on having them with him.

He'd never been separated from them and couldn't imagine being so for months. And now his baby was in danger.

Tears filled Mrs. Weston's eyes. "I won't be responsible for a child who runs off. You'll have to find someone else to look after her. If you find her." She turned on her heel and strode away.

The woman had seemed competent, but now he wondered. She couldn't even keep track of one little girl.

The lunch bell rang, and men gathered around. One of them asked, "What is it, Thompson?"

"My daughter is missing."

Soon, the men he'd worked with for only a few hours had formed search parties of twos.

"But it's your lunch break." These men needed the rest after how hard they worked. Arduous physical labor. These men didn't even know him, yet they were not only willing to help, they were eager.

"A child is missing. Lunch can wait."

As the men dispersed, the foreman called out, "Be back by the end of the break!"

The man who had swiftly organized searchers paired up with him, and they headed back to Mrs. Weston's home. The man held out his hand. "I'm Marcus."

Lindley took the offered hand. "Lindley."

"How old is your little one?"

"Four."

Marcus shook his head. "Too young to be off on her own in a town she doesn't know. And too young for school."

"School?" Lindley spun around and took off running.

Marcus caught up to him. "You have an idea?"

"She whined last night and again this morning about not being able to go to school with her brother." When the one-room schoolhouse was in sight, he ran faster and burst through the door.

All heads turned. All eyes were on him.

His attention was captured for a moment by the lovely green-eyed teacher. "My daughter. Is she here?"

Miss Greene pointed to the front row.

Dora turned and waved. "I'm in school, Papa."

Lindley hurried to the front and scooped her up in his arms. "You're *safe*."

Marcus clasped a hand on his shoulder. "Your daughter?"

Lindley nodded.

"I'll tell the others and call off the search," Marcus said as he turned to leave.

Lindley hoped Marcus and the other men still had time to eat their lunches.

"Search?" Miss Greene asked. "Dora said the woman couldn't look after her. I thought you'd sent her here."

"No, she ran off." He pulled Dora away from his shoulder so he could look her in the face. "Why did you run off?"

Dora pointed her finger and looked indignant. "I wanted to go to school." As if that was a perfectly acceptable reason for running off without telling Mrs. Weston.

"Don't you point your little finger at me. You never ever run away from the person I have set to look after you. Do you understand?"

Dora nodded. "But I had to go to school. Teacher said I could be here."

Miss Greene nodded over Dora's head so he could see but not his daughter.

Lindley got lost in the teacher's green eyes but quickly shook himself free. He'd come to find his daughter. And come to Roche Harbor for a job, nothing more. The schoolteacher had her own job to tend to. "I'm sorry for disturbing your class. If it truly is all right for Dora to stay—but just for today—that would be helpful. I *will* make other arrangements for her care."

"You do what you feel is best for your daughter. But it is quite all right for her to stay if you choose. She and Aggie are getting on well."

He hated to reward his daughter's disobedience but had few options. "Thank you." But this teacher had her hands full already with her classroom of all different ages. He would try to convince Mrs. Weston to take Dora during the day. He headed back to work with visions of the red-haired schoolteacher dancing in his head. Her sweet smile and agreeable nature warmed his heart.

As the other students filed out the door at the end of the school day, Bridget asked Gabe and Dora to stay. She squatted down to the boy's level. "Do you and your sister have someplace to go after school?"

The boy shrugged. "Mrs. Weston's?"

She knew the woman. She loved babies but could be impatient with older children, especially ones who asserted their own wills. So if Mrs. Weston wasn't able to watch Dora, then she wasn't likely able to watch both children after school until their father got off work. "How would the two of you like to come to my house until your father is done with work and comes to get you?"

Both children nodded. Gabe beamed a smile, and Dora hugged her.

"Let me write a note for your father. Then we will leave. Go ahead and take a seat until I'm ready." She wrote the note, telling Mr. Thompson that she had taken his children home with her. And then she wrote her address.

Oh, dear. What if Mr. Thompson couldn't read? Just because he sent his children to school, and Gabe was obviously bright and could read, didn't mean he could. She had several students with more education than their parents, parents who'd never gone to school and couldn't read. So she drew a map to her house on the bottom of the paper.

"Let's go." She gathered up her satchel and ushered the children out and to her house three blocks away.

Dusk loomed as Lindley approached the schoolhouse. When Mrs. Weston had quit this morning, he hadn't thought about where his children would go after school until he'd finished work. What would his sisters say about that? He wouldn't tell them. He hoped Gabe and Dora were still at the school.

The pretty teacher would be none too pleased with him for being so negligent and for the imposition it must have caused her. After being at the school all day with children, she likely welcomed the break from them in the evenings.

A sheet of paper addressed to him was attached to the schoolhouse door. He yanked it free and read it. So she'd taken them home. Well, at least she wasn't stuck at the school. He was once more in her debt.

He did hope she was trustworthy. After Mrs. Weston, he just wasn't too confident. And mining companies weren't known for being picky when choosing a teacher. Any willing person was generally hired.

He trotted off in the direction of the teacher's house.

When a knock sounded on the door, Bridget opened it. Her breath caught. Though dirty from a day of hard work, Mr. Thompson was still quite handsome. Even though she knew he was coming, and dirty as he was, the sight of him caused her heart to gallop ahead. "Mr. Thompson, I'm glad you made it. Did you have any trouble finding my house?"

He held up the note she had left pinned to the schoolhouse. "Thank you for the map. I don't know the streets yet."

That didn't tell her if he could read or not. Many illiterate people were good at covering up their deficiency.

He cleared his throat. "I am so sorry for inconveniencing you."

"It was no trouble. You have sweet children. Please come in." She stepped back.

"I'm sweaty and dirty. I just came for my children."

How considerate. He'd obviously been raised by a mother who taught him manners.

He looked past her. "Gabe. Dora. Time to go. Thank Miss Greene."

His son stayed seated at the table. "Miss Greene invited us for supper."

"Gabe, don't argue. We've caused Miss Greene enough trouble."

Gabe's shoulders slumped as he stood. "But she cooked fried chicken."

Dora beamed up at her father. "I set a plate for you." She pointed to a place at the table.

If he went home now, he'd still have to prepare supper. It would be a long while before they ate. And he'd already had a long day at work. And most of all, Bridget looked forward to having the company. She wanted to intervene and try to convince him to stay, but she held her tongue. From behind the children, Bridget nodded to Mr. Thompson to let him know it was truly all right with her.

"I don't want eggs again," Gabe said.

Dora folded her arms and shook her head. "And I don't want any more pancakes. I set a place for you, Papa."

"I'm sorry for causing an issue," Bridget said. "Not knowing how late you'd be, I didn't want the children to go hungry."

Dora pressed her hands together. "Please."

Bridget could visibly see Mr. Thompson's resolve crumbling even under the grime on his face. "That was thoughtful of you, but we couldn't impose." Though his words said his family would not stay, his stance and gaze said he didn't have the strength to refuse the invitation. His stomach growled.

Bridget pretended she hadn't heard. "May we speak outside?"

Mr. Thompson moved back, and she stepped out onto the porch. He looked inside. "You two stay there for a minute." He closed the door.

"The food is already prepared, and there is plenty, so it really is no imposition. But it is completely up to you. If you say you must go, I will shoo your children out without another argument. But I would enjoy the company."

His stomach growled again, and his mouth twitched in recognition. "It does smell awfully good." He looked down at his hands, which were nearly black with dirt. "But I'm too grimy."

"It's just dirt. I have soap and water."

Still he hesitated. "Are you sure it's not an imposition?"

He wasn't one of her students whom she could order to do as she bid. She nodded. "If a little dirt was going to bother me, I shouldn't be teaching in a mining town."

He finally relented.

She opened the door and stepped inside ahead of him.

He shifted his gaze from Gabe's eager face to Dora's and back. "Since supper is all cooked and a place is set for us, we can stay."

His children cheered.

He rolled up his shirtsleeves and washed his hands and arms up to his elbows twice, as well as his face and neck. She doubted most miners would think to wash so thoroughly or even think to scrub their neck. Who was this man? She sat at the table with the children and waited for him to finish.

Soon he sat at the end opposite her. He reached for his children's hands and they his. Gabe and Dora each held a hand stretched out to her.

She took the children's hands. Never in her life had she had anyone say grace at her table besides her.

Mr. Thompson gave her a nod. "I would be honored to say the blessing. You did do all the work."

She agreed and bowed her head.

"Father in heaven, we thank You for another day of life and breath in these frail bodies we live in. We ask blessings upon Miss Greene for her kindness and generosity. And we thank You for the bounty You have provided. Nourish our bodies with this food and our souls with Your presence. In Jesus's name, amen."

She had never heard anyone pray for her by name. It was as though God had reached down and caressed her soul. Nor had anyone thanked her so generously for doing so little. Moved by the prayer, she had to blink back tears as she lifted her head.

Lindley set his fork down and sat back in the chair at Miss Greene's table. He couldn't remember the last time a meal had been this satisfying. Not that he hadn't had tasty meals, even in the recent past. This was something more. And for some reason, he felt as though the something more must be Miss Greene herself. It must be her consideration for his children. Not only was she kind and generous, but smart—she would have to be to be a teacher—and patient and…and… He gazed at her.

No. He wouldn't focus on her physical attributes. People were more than how they looked. Her green gaze captured him. Eyes the color of the forests all across the San Juan Islands. And chestnut hair that flickered with bits of red in the lamplight. He couldn't deny that she was lovely.

And she said she prayed before meals, so she was likely a Christian, too. But he couldn't figure out why she was almost in tears after grace. That would be something he might never know. It would be rude to ask directly about something so personal.

"Supper was delicious." He regretted what he must say next but said it anyway. "We'll get out of your way now. Time to go, children." He leaned forward to stand.

She spoke quickly. "You don't have to go. We haven't had dessert yet."

Dora clapped her hands. "Yay! Dessert!"

Dessert? "Dessert would be nice." He settled back down but then stood fully when she leaped from her chair.

"It's nothing fancy. Just applesauce." She returned to the table with a jar. "I canned it last fall."

He had always loved applesauce. How long had it been since he'd had any? Eight, maybe nine years. Before he was married. "Cinnamon?"

"Yes. I hope that's all right. Since I just make it for myself, I always add cinnamon. But I might have a jar of peaches or cherries if you prefer."

She seemed nervous.

"I love cinnamon."

She gripped the ring of the lid and tried to twist it off without success. "These are difficult sometimes."

He held out his hand. "Allow me."

She handed it over without a fuss. His older half sister would have struggled with the lid until her hands bled, wanting to prove herself capable.

Grasping the jar and the ring lid, he twisted. The ring slid in his hand. He tightened his grip and tried again, still without success. *Oh, please don't let me fail. Not in front of her. Not with a silly jar.* He took a deep breath and jerked the ring and jar in opposite directions. The ring broke free.

Dora clapped again. "Papa is strongerest."

Setting the jar on the table, he took his table knife, put the edge under the lip of the lid and lifted, breaking the seal. Air sucked into the jar with a gasp, releasing the lid.

After the large jar of applesauce had been consumed, he said, "We really must be going. I need to get Gabe and Dora to bed. Children, carry your plates over to the sink."

Gabe and Dora did as he bid them. Dora's eyes were already drooping. She held out her arms, and he picked her up. Her head lolled onto his shoulder.

At the door, he said, "Supper was delicious. We'll reciprocate."

"You don't have to do that."

He supposed she thought he was like all the other miners and couldn't afford it. He would prove her wrong. "I insist. It won't be as tasty as your cooking, but we do all right. And you don't have to worry about my children after school hours. I will make arrangements for them." He couldn't believe his earlier lack of judgment.

"I'm sure they could walk home with the Bennetts' children and stay there until you are off work."

He knew Gary Bennett, the one who had trained him today. He was a good man. "Thank you."

That had been a better meal than he'd ever cooked. After the fuss he'd made to his family about him being able to care for his children, they would say that this proved he couldn't.

But there was no shame in accepting help now and then.

And Miss Greene had been very accommodating and generous.

Chapter 3

The next day, when Bridget welcomed her students, she was not surprised to see Dora Thompson among them. Bridget knew it had been too late by the time the Thompsons had left her house for Mr. Thompson to find someone to look after the girl.

The four-year-old marched up to her desk as though she had always been in school. "Papa said I could come to school as long as I don't cause no trouble and you say I can."

Bridget nodded to the girl. "Go sit with Aggie."

Dora twirled around and flounced over to where Aggie sat. Aggie broke into a big smile.

Yesterday had actually been a little easier than usual with Dora and Aggie keeping each other occupied. She'd had to warn them only twice to keep their voices down. Whenever Bridget threatened to separate them, they fell into a hushed whisper. Until yesterday, she had never had a day where Aggie didn't come up to her desk at least once to complain she was bored. And occasionally danced in the corner.

But Bridget could see that now that the girls were friends, their play had become more animated throughout the day. And even though they were as quiet as church mice, they distracted not only the students but Bridget, as well.

Bridget would have to find a solution if she was going to get any teaching done. She dismissed the students for morning recess and sat out on the stoop to watch them while reading the next hour's lessons.

She decided that she needed to give the two girls more structure in the school day. Where Aggie could be somber most of the day, content to draw and page through books she couldn't actually read, as a pair, they were a little more active. Her other students had their subjects to occupy them. Reading, writing, 'rithmetic, spelling, history and geography.

What "subjects" would four-year-olds be able to take on? She could start them on letter recognition and tracing letters. But that would not occupy them all day. She would have to come up with more things for them to do. But she couldn't let it take too much time away from her other students.

During the second morning session, the letter recognition and tracing adequately kept the two little girls busy. After lunch, she laid out a quilt in the corner and made them lie down. They both fell asleep within minutes. After the afternoon recess, she had them draw.

That evening, she devised lesson plans for the whole day for the pair. She would need to enlist the help of some of the older students as she did with the first- and second-graders.

The next few days scurried by with both the Thompson children in her class. They settled into the school routine and walked home with the Bennett children.

The students she had chosen to work with Aggie and Dora were doing wonderfully. They read to the girls and taught them the alphabet, numbers, counting, colors and shapes. After lunch, the two girls always fell asleep. All was working splendidly.

* * *

On his fourth day of work, Lindley took his lunch and ate under a stand of trees in sight of the schoolhouse. He scanned the children until he saw Gabe with three other boys about his age. They stood in a circle playing battledore and shuttlecock. Even when he missed the shuttlecock with his paddle, he seemed happy.

Dora and another little girl played together. What had his daughter said her friend's name was? Yes. Aggie. They held hands and spun around in a circle until they both fell down.

He smiled at the pair.

Miss Greene sat on the steps of the school, eating her lunch. Maybe he should approach and sit with her while they both ate.

No. That was silly. She had her job and he had his.

He could see that his children were fine. He should head back to the mining company to finish his boiled eggs and bread with the other men. But he didn't.

When he finally did head back to work, the lunch break had ended. He hoped not too long ago.

"Thompson!" the foreman called.

Mr. Brady's scowl told him that lunch must have been over for some time.

He trotted to the man. "I'm sorry about being late. It won't happen again."

"You're right it won't. There are plenty of other men who would love to have your job, who will be on time and work harder than you. I spoke with Keen and told him I didn't think you were working out and he should fire your worthless carcass."

He'd spoken to the mine manager?

"He wants to see you. And if I'm real lucky, I won't be seeing you again."

Lindley wouldn't mind not seeing Brady again, but he couldn't get fired. He hustled to Mr. Keen's office and knocked.

"Come in."

Lindley opened the door and entered the dimly lit, ten-by-ten room. "You asked to see me?"

Keen frowned. "Close the door."

Lindley did and moved toward the straight-backed chair opposite the desk cluttered with rock samples and papers.

"I didn't invite you to sit."

Lindley straightened. "I'm sorry—"

"I'll tell you when you can speak." Keen paused and took a deep breath. "Do you want this to work?"

"Yes, sir." Lindley desperately needed this job to go well.

"You wandered off during the lunch break?"

"I didn't think I had to stay on the premises."

"You came back late. You get lost?"

"No. I didn't realize how long I was gone."

"Brady already doesn't like you. Says you aren't cut out for the work. He wants me to fire—how did he put it—your namby-pamby carcass."

He couldn't do that. "I'll work harder and won't ever be late again."

"Maybe a week in the mine will give you an appreciation for working the kilns."

"You can't—"

"I don't want to hear it. Get yourself a cap lamp and sledgehammer. Then report to Ross. I think it will be real good for you to see what goes on underground. Now go."

Lindley wasn't sure arguing would do any good, so he turned and left. He would work harder than any two men down there and be back up top in a week. Or less.

All this trouble because of a woman. He had to keep his head on straight. Focus on the job.

He grabbed the equipment and reported to Ross.

That evening, exhausted, he fell into bed but was roused awake sometime later by Gabe and Dora climbing into bed with him. That was when he heard the rain pelting the flimsy roof. "Did the storm scare you?"

Gabe shook his head against Lindley's side. "Our bed's wet."

"Dora?"

"I didn't do it. The rain comed in."

Lindley sat up, climbed over Gabe and off the bed. The bare wood floor was cold on his feet. He pulled the clean, warm quilt over their shoulders. Thank God it was dry.

Across the room, rain dripped down in two places on the straw mattress. He pulled the mattress to the middle of the room to keep it from getting any wetter. He placed a pan under each of the drips and put a bowl under a third drip in front of the door.

The mining-company houses, besides being small, had been built fast and cheap out of flimsy materials. He would see what could be done about them.

He lay awake most of the night, listening to the rain drip, drip, dripping inside the house.

Though his children didn't have school on Saturday, he still had to work. Mrs. Bennett welcomed Gabe and Dora for the day. She said that two more running around would hardly be noticed.

Sunday was a blessed reprieve. He did not want to get out of bed, but he must. His children needed to be fed, and they all needed to get dressed for church.

Even with fog hanging over the town and harbor, a lot of people lingered in the churchyard. He didn't see the schoolteacher. When piano music filtered outside, the crowd moved toward and in through the door. He found a place in the back pew just big enough for him and Gabe to squeeze into, so he pulled Dora onto his lap, causing his already sore muscles to protest.

He searched the pews for Miss Greene's auburn hair but couldn't spot her. She'd said she prayed before meals, so why wasn't she in church? Surely she went. It wasn't as if there was another option in town.

After three hymns, the pastor dismissed the pianist. Miss Greene stood and glanced about the filled room before sitting in the front pew. He hadn't thought to look for her at the piano. But now he knew.

Bridget returned to the piano for the concluding hymn, glancing once more about the room but not seeing Mr. Thompson and his children. With his prayer the other night at supper, she was sure he would be a churchgoer.

The morning had dawned to heavy fog. If a person didn't know where he was going, he could easily get disoriented. Had Mr. Thompson and his children gotten lost this morning? She hadn't seen them before the service started, and now it would be impolite to turn to look for them. She did hope they were all safe and well.

After the congregation finished singing, she continued to play while people filed out. She closed the hymnal and lowered the cover to the piano keys.

Upon standing, she sucked in a breath.

Mr. Thompson sat in the last pew with his children. He *had* been here.

She smoothed her dress, picked up her hat and shawl from the front pew and made her way down the aisle. As she approached, he stood, and her insides did that funny little thing they did when he was near.

He dipped his head. "Miss Greene."

She wrapped her shawl around her shoulders. "Mr. Thompson. Hello, Gabe. Hello, Dora."

"Hi, Teacher." Dora held her arms up to her.

"Dora, no."

As he was speaking, Bridget set her hat on her head, leaving the ties hanging, and lifted the girl, settling the child on her hip. "I don't mind." One day, she hoped to have children of her own. But at twenty-five, how likely was that? Each passing year plucked away at her hope like removing petals from a flower one by one and letting them fall to the ground. So she loved her students as her own. "Did you enjoy the service?"

"It was nice. I stayed because I wanted to talk to you."

"Oh." She cringed inside at her impolite response. What could he possibly want to talk to her about? Certainly not that he had the same strange feeling in his stomach that she had when she was near him.

"I wanted to know how Gabe is doing in school and if it is working out having Dora in class."

Of course he would want to talk about his children. She was such a silly ninny.

"If Dora is too much trouble, I can find someone to look after her. I won't have her being a bother to you."

How considerate of him.

Dora rubbed one of Bridget's satin ties on her cheek.

"Dora is no trouble. She and Aggie keep each other occupied. I have some of the older children helping them learn the alphabet and numbers." She glanced down at the boy. "Gabe is settling in just fine. Aren't you?"

Gabe beamed up at her and nodded.

Bridget noticed how striking Mr. Thompson looked in a clean crisp shirt and pressed trousers. Gabe's and Dora's clothes were quite nice for miner's children. How could he afford them? Then she realized that a missionary barrel with discarded clothes could easily account for their wardrobes.

Mr. Thompson reached out blistered hands and took Dora. Hands that hadn't previously been used to hard labor. "Well, I appreciate all you do in teaching the children."

Her arms felt empty without the child. She walked out with them, the last four in the building.

"We won't keep you any longer. Good day, Miss Greene." He tipped his hat, and they walked away.

Those children were fortunate to have been the exact right size for those clothes.

Quite fortunate indeed.

There seemed to be more to the man than met the eye. She'd best stay clear of Mr. Thompson until she figured out what.

Chapter 4

After full days of breaking rocks, Lindley had little energy in the evenings to give his children much attention. For the following week, it was all he could do to fix simple suppers, get Gabe and Dora settled down each night and fall into bed himself.

He had never done so much physical labor. Swinging a sledgehammer and hauling rocks were not jobs he would choose. The labor was both a blessing and a curse. A curse for how tired and sore he was, and a blessing because it afforded him no time or energy to contemplate the pretty schoolteacher.

But tonight, even overwhelmed with exhaustion, he stared at Gabe's paper and knew it wasn't right. Fifty-seven out of one hundred points? How dare that small-town teacher judge his son's work unworthy just because he was a miner's kid. Gabe took after his mother and was bright beyond his years. Lindley would just give that teacher a piece of his mind.

Bridget sat in front of her fire, stitching quilt blocks. She had half of them completed for her wandering-star quilt.

Someone banged on her door. She startled and dropped a block on the floor. She picked it up and set the quilting in the sewing basket beside her chair.

Who could be at her door at this hour? She never had

evening visitors. She crossed to the window to peer out. Mr. Thompson stood on her porch. The sight of that man sent her insides into a tizzy. No, just the thought of him. What was wrong with her?

She opened the door. "Good evening, Mr. Thompson."

"Evening." He stepped back and swung one hand out. "May I have a word with you?" His lips pressed into a thin line.

What had upset him? Hopefully nothing wrong with Gabe or Dora. She grabbed her wool shawl off the hook by the door and wrapped herself in it before stepping out onto the porch. The cold April air seeped through the shawl. She would invite him in her small house if it wasn't just the two of them. "What's the matter?"

He glared at her and then held out some sheets of paper, shaking them. "*This* is what is the matter."

Bridget took his son's paper. A story. Gabe had gotten a poor grade. She was glad Mr. Thompson had come. She wanted to speak to him about it.

He continued. "Do you think that miners are stupid or something?"

She opened her mouth to say she didn't believe that at all, but he didn't give her a chance.

"That you don't have to treat our children fairly?"

Now, that wasn't true either. But he didn't appear to be interested in a conversation, just his unwarranted opinions of her. Good. His ire, misplaced as it was, would squelch her wayward heart. But his protectiveness of his son only endeared him all the more to her.

"You're more educated, so you scorn the rest of us? The upper crust looking down on the poor working folks, thinking you're better."

She didn't think herself better. And being the school-teacher in a mining town was hardly the "upper crust." If there was a hierarchy, schoolteacher would be only half a step above, if that.

"My son is very smart. At his last school, he received all top marks. Even for work above his grade. And you have the audacity to give him a score like that? I question whether you are even qualified to be a teacher. I'm going to have the school board look into your credentials. You are not going to treat my son or any of the other children in this manner."

His words were meant to hurt her, but instead, she saw his pain in thinking his child was being unfairly treated. So she let him blow off steam.

His tirade slowed, and he began repeating himself. He clamped his teeth together, stopping his flow. "Well, don't you have anything to say for yourself?"

"If you're ready to listen."

Breathing heavily from his verbal attack, he gave a curt nod.

"I do *not* think I am better than anyone else. We are all equal in God's eyes. The children in this town, *all* the children, are dear to me." She had an extra-soft spot for the miners' children because most of them didn't have hope for a better future than their parents. One hard life handed down from generation to generation like a family heirloom.

"Yet you grade a miner's child more harshly?"

She held out the paper in question. "Did you read your son's story?"

He squinted at the paper but didn't take it. "I don't have to. He was reading by age four. He is intelligent."

"I agree. He is very intelligent. That's why his story bothers me." She continued to hold the paper out. "Read your son's story. And if you don't agree with my grade, I'll change it." She still wasn't sure if he *could* read.

He snatched the paper and began reading. "This can't

be." His pinched face relaxed a little at a time until his lips parted. "This can't be." He shuffled to the next page. "This can't be Gabe's."

And yet it was. She mentally sighed with relief. He understood.

He fisted his hand around the corner of the pages and shook them. "Gabe writes better than this. He wrote better than this at age five. Words he knows are grossly misspelled. And there is no regard for punctuation or grammar."

"Is that not Gabe's name and penmanship?"

He let out a long breath that seemed to take any remaining anger with it. "It is." He turned and sat on the porch step. "I don't understand."

Finally, he was ready to listen. She sat next to him. But not too close, though she would have liked to. She shifted sideways to face him. "I believe Gabe is vying for my attention. That's why his work has suddenly become poor, and he's been misbehaving in class."

He squinted at her. "Misbehaving? Gabe?"

She nodded. "He has seen other students get attention by causing trouble. And others need extra help from me on their lessons. That's why, when he acts up, I make him stand in the back of the schoolroom, away from me. And why I didn't talk to him about his work. I didn't want to reward him for this kind of behavior. I was going to speak with you about his schoolwork performance as well as his conduct."

"He's never done anything like this before."

"In less than two weeks in my classroom, he figured out how things work and devised a plan he thought would get him what he wanted. Your son is *very* bright for a seven-year-old."

Mr. Thompson stood and turned to face her. "I'm sorry

for making unfounded accusations against you. *My* comportment this evening has been deplorable."

She stood, as well. "You were looking out for your son. I'm glad you care so much about how he is doing in school. A lot of the parents don't. They are either too tired from working or don't understand the value of an education for their children."

He held up the paper. "You graded him too kindly on this. I'll see to it that Gabe rewrites this story correctly. Good evening." He strode away.

She stared after him. Not only could Mr. Thompson read, but he knew rules of grammar and spelling. He spoke like a person with more than a rudimentary education, using words such as *deplorable*, *audacity* and *comportment*. And yet he was a miner. Certainly he could acquire a better position.

She went back inside to the warmth of her house.

Mr. Thompson didn't behave in a manner like any other miner she knew. The man was an enigma.

The heat of his embarrassment kept Lindley warm all the way home. He should have read Gabe's paper before accusing Miss Greene of bias. She would think poorly of him after this. That caused an ache in his chest. Though he knew he shouldn't, he liked Miss Greene. And now she would never think of him as a potential suitor.

Suitor? Posh. What was *he* thinking? He had neither the time nor the inclination to pursue a woman. That was what had made his first marriage so perfect. Prearranged, no courting. But he had to admit that he felt something for the schoolteacher. A pulling. A longing. A need. Something he hadn't felt for his late wife, Doreen, whom he had come to love.

He'd left Gabe and Dora at the Bennetts' before going

to confront Miss Greene. He collected his children and headed to his own undersized dwelling two shacks down. How the miner families lived year in and year out in these houses that were little more than tents was beyond him. Some of them looked ready to fall down even though they were only a few years old. He would see what he could do to improve the living conditions. If a worker felt safe and content at home, he would perform better on the job.

He set Gabe at the rough-plank table with his story. "We will talk about this after I put Dora to bed."

Dora gave her brother a knowing glance and then went down quickly. Lindley sat across the table from his son. "Why did you purposely write this poorly?"

Gabe shrugged.

"Did you do poorly because you wanted Miss Greene's attention? So she would have to help you?"

His son shrugged again.

"Gabe?"

His son sighed. "She helps students who can't do the work."

"But you *can* do the work. Doing poorly on purpose is just like lying. Do you want Miss Greene to think of you as a liar? Someone she can't trust?"

Gabe shook his head.

"You aren't going to do this again, are you?"

Gabe shook his head again.

"You will stay inside at recess tomorrow and rewrite this story."

His son had his head down and spoke in a sad voice. "All right."

"And Miss Greene says you have been misbehaving in class. You will stop that at once. If I hear of one more instance, I'll send you to stay with your aunt Alice."

Gabe jerked his head up. "I'll be good."

"Very well. Now off to bed." Lindley's sister wasn't bad, but she would make him toe the line. She made sure her children behaved and would have more time than Lindley to give Gabe attention. But sending his son away would be a last resort.

Gabe scuttled off to bed.

Lindley believed the schoolteacher was right. Gabe wanted her attention. He had been old enough to remember his mother, unlike Dora. His boy probably missed having a mother to soothe his fevered brow and tend to his scraped knees.

Lindley could understand that. Didn't he, as well, long for the teacher's attention? Yes, he had to admit he did. So maybe he should stop fighting himself and do something about it. Let her know he was interested in her. More than just as his children's teacher. If she didn't return his interest, then he would think of her no more in that manner.

The next morning, he walked his children to the schoolhouse early to talk to Miss Greene before he had to be at the lime mine. Only two more days of swinging the hammer. She wasn't there yet, so he let himself and his children inside.

He crossed to the potbelly stove and stirred the banked fire with a small chunk of wood until the coals glowed. He threw in some kindling and blew on it until the fire jumped to life and caught.

"Oh, Mr. Thompson."

Lindley straightened, and his insides twisted at the sight of the teacher. He took a calming breath and crossed to her. "Miss Greene, Gabe is rewriting his story. If he doesn't finish before school starts, he is to remain indoors for recess to complete it."

"That's acceptable."

"I also wanted to apologize once again for my behavior last night. It was uncalled for."

"All is forgiven." She set her books and papers on a nearby desk. "Please don't worry over it any further."

He stepped forward. "I was wondering—I mean my children and I were wondering if you would join us for a picnic lunch after church on Sunday."

"That's not necessary. I appreciate your concern for your children."

His mouth went dry, and his heart felt as though it were shrinking. She didn't want to go with him? She didn't like him, as well? Disappointment stabbed him in the chest.

"I promised to reciprocate the favor of a meal. I must insist. My children will be sorely disappointed if you don't join us."

She removed her bonnet. "If you insist, I would love to join you. All of you."

He had pressed the matter and even used his children to get her to agree. And now she was only going out of obligation. What had gotten into him?

Chapter 5

Sitting in the first row at church on Sunday, Bridget pulled the edge of her handkerchief through her fingers. Down one side, around the corner, down the next, around and around the square of cloth. She tried to focus on the sermon but had difficulty concentrating.

She wasn't sure if today's picnic was simply reciprocating a meal, or if it meant something more. She fancied the idea of it being more—what woman wouldn't want to know she was attractive to a handsome man?—but she knew she should discourage any interest from Mr. Thompson. And she toward him.

At least until she could figure him out.

She heard the minister clear his throat and shifted her gaze to him.

He was staring at her and tilted his head toward the piano.

She went to the instrument immediately, embarrassed to have been so distracted as to miss her cue. After the final hymn, she played it through again while some of the congregation left. She closed the piano and gathered her things.

This morning several clusters of people lingered.

Mr. Thompson waited with his children in a back pew until she came down the aisle to where he stood. "Good morning, Miss Greene. Beautiful day for a picnic."

She stepped into the pew row to get out of the way of others now ready to leave. "Then the fog has burned off?"

He leaned down a bit to peer out the window. "It still looks pretty thick."

Then what had he meant by "beautiful day for a picnic"? "If the weather is too much, we can put off the picnic to another day."

"If Islanders put off things until days were clear, precious little would get accomplished. Rain may dampen things, but this is just a little fog."

It was a lot of fog, but she liked his attitude. And his use of "Islanders" meant he was likely a native of San Juan Island or had lived here most of his life. She patted the handle of her basket. "I baked cookies for dessert."

Dora jumped up and down where she stood on the pew seat. "What kind? What kind?"

"It's a surprise. You'll have to wait until after lunch." She turned her focus back to Mr. Thompson. "Where are we going to picnic?"

"Well, I was hoping you would have some suggestions. I don't know the area yet."

"Very well, then. Shall we go?" She knew just the spot. One of her favorites, in view of the harbor, but not too close to the water to put the children in danger.

As the afternoon wore on, the fog didn't so much lift as get swallowed up in a darkening sky. It would rain soon. But she didn't want to leave. She was enjoying the afternoon with this enigmatic man and his children.

There had been miners before who had shown an interest in her, but none of them had given her that strange feeling inside that this one did. Maybe it was simply the mystery about him that piqued her interest. That he could be so much more than a simple miner if only given the chance. Or maybe he was more. Either way, she needed to hold on to her heart.

The food had already been packed away when the first drops fell. She sprang to her feet, gathered up the two baskets and the beige quilt, and raced for the covering of the trees. She stopped and turned around. "You're going to get wet."

Mr. Thompson stood a few feet away in the rain with his children. "It's just a little water."

Dora held up her arms.

Mr. Thompson scooped her up and spun around. The man was dancing in the rain with his daughter. And enjoying it. He motioned to her to join them.

That was when she first noticed the limp in Mr. Thompson's left leg. Had he injured himself at work? She hoped he was all right.

Gabe clapped his hands and danced around, too.

Watching Mr. Thompson out there with his children told Bridget that this was simply the reciprocation of supper. For if he were trying to woo her, he would not be dancing and laughing in the rain but trying to impress her. All this "rain dance" accomplished was to make him more appealing.

Then Gabe came over and grabbed her hand. "Come on, Teacher."

Bridget resisted, but Gabe insisted. She gave in, letting the baskets and quilt drop, and allowed herself to be pulled out into the rain.

She cringed at the drops hitting her and soaking into her clothes.

Mr. Thompson set Dora down. He took one of each of his children's hands, and they reached for Bridget's. Little wet fingers in hers. Dancing in a circle, Bridget still hoped not to get too wet. The desire to run back to the covering of the trees skittered through her mind. But it was already too late, and she didn't want to disappoint the children.

Tilting back her head, she let the rain refresh her face. When she did, she felt lighter and began to laugh. She hadn't had this much fun since she was a child. Her parents would have a fit if they could see her now.

How could a woman not lose her heart to this man? He loved his children and apparently loved life, not letting hardships get him down.

The continuing rain dripped from Lindley's hat and hands and face, though it had slowed to more of a drizzle. He picked up the quilt from the protection of the trees. It had remained relatively dry. He held it open to Miss Greene. "To keep you warm."

"Oh, wrap the children in it. I would hate for them to get sick."

She was right, of course, but he wanted her warm, as well. He would hate for *her* to get sick. He folded the quilt once and wrapped it around Gabe and Dora together so that it covered their heads as well as their bodies.

The foursome set out for Miss Greene's house, their feet making squishy sounds on the soggy earth.

Concerned for Miss Greene, he said, "Are you warm enough?"

"Yes, I'm fine." She pulled her shawl a little tighter.

Though her wrap looked to be warm, possibly wool, he wasn't so sure it was all that much help as soaked as it was. "I'm sorry for getting you all wet."

Her mouth turned up at the corners. "Are you in control of the weather? Did you *make* it rain?"

"No, but still, it's my fault."

"I don't recall you dragging me out from under the trees."

Obviously, she wasn't going to blame him. She had been reluctant, even squinting as the first drops had hit her. "No, but my son did."

His children waddled together a foot or so ahead of him, bundled in the tan quilt.

"And I could have easily outmuscled him."

Gabe jostled his sister. "Pick up your side or you'll trip."

Dora did her best to comply.

Miss Greene smiled at the children's backs and continued, "You looked as though you were having a lot of fun. Carefree."

Not exactly carefree. "I still feel bad." Playing in the rain was not the way to impress a lady. If his sisters found out, they would give him an earful. Each of them. He didn't have that many ears.

She didn't seem to mind the rain at all now. "Have you always loved the rain?"

Loved the rain? No, he didn't love the rain. More like a tolerance. "Not particularly."

"But you were having such fun."

He had to work at it.

Dora tripped and landed on her hands and knees on the muddy ground.

"Dora!" Gabe stopped. "I told you so."

His daughter whimpered.

Lindley helped Dora to her feet and wiped her hands on his pants to clean off most of the mud. Dora wrapped her arms around his neck, and he stood, holding her.

Gabe tugged the quilt tighter, apparently glad to have it to himself.

Lindley picked up the conversation where it had been left hanging when Dora fell. "When I was a boy, I didn't mind one way or the other. Rain was rain. I didn't like it when my mother wouldn't let me go outside because of it."

"So what changed?"

He wasn't sure he should tell her, but at the same time he wanted to explain his strange behavior so she didn't think him touched in the head. "When I was twelve, I ran away when it was raining and slipped over a cliff. I was trapped for hours. It was dark, and I was so cold."

"How awful. What caused you to run out into the night?"

He shifted his daughter in his arms. "It was the afternoon and light out. I was angry with my father for being unfair to my older sister. He hated the English, and Rachel was in love with a British officer. So I ran off. It was stupid, really."

"You must have been so frightened." Her gentle, sympathetic tone comforted him.

He wanted to push back a lock of wet hair from her face, but knew that would be inappropriate, so he did so to Dora instead. "I thought I was going to die. I tried to pretend I wasn't as scared as I really was. I used to have terrible nightmares on stormy nights." Used to? He still did. Doreen had been good at soothing him when he cried out in the night.

"I don't understand how that relates to dancing in the rain."

"First of all, I don't dance. *Playing* in the rain is like a celebration. The storm didn't get the better of me. I lived."

She stopped just short of her porch steps and stared at him.

She must think him daft for sure. He wished he'd kept quiet about the whole story. Said something feeble, like he knew his children would enjoy it, and brushed it off. But her compassion and interest had drawn it out of him.

"That is so inspiring."

"It is?" How could being terrified of rain be inspiring?

"You took something that was horrible and turned it into something wonderful."

It had been Doreen who had helped him face his fear. She'd taken him out in a storm and had him close his eyes. Smell the freshness it brought. Feel it on his face. Washing away his fear. "I never wanted Gabe and Dora to be afraid like I was."

She touched Dora's arm. "I think you have succeeded marvelously. Would you like to come in and warm up before you continue on home?"

He would very much like to stay. "Thank you, but no. I want to get Gabe and Dora out of their wet clothes." He tipped his hat with his free hand, scooped up his son still wrapped in the quilt and then headed for home.

His mouth pulled into a smile. She thought his dancing in the rain was inspiring and wonderful. Yes, he'd been *dancing* with his children.

Chapter 6

Two days later, Lindley met with Marcus after supper. "Thank you for coming."

Marcus stood, leaning against the corner of Lindley's company shanty. "Sure. What's with all the secrecy?"

"I have a matter I wish to discuss with you. You know the men better than I do."

Marcus clasped him on the shoulder in a friendly manner. "Are you worried the men don't like you? In time, you will know them all well and they you."

"That's not it. Yes, in time. But I want to know what grievances they have."

Marcus jerked his hand away as though jabbed with a hot poker. "Grievances?"

"Things at work they would like to see changed. Like the houses the company provides. They are only slightly better than no roof at all. My roof has at least three leaks. Every time it rains, the inside is as wet as the outside. I want to talk to the site manager to get things improved for everyone. If we go in with one thing we want changed, we won't get it. But if we have five, we might get two. Three if we're lucky."

Marcus stepped back. "We don't want no trouble. This is good honest work."

He didn't understand Marcus's reluctance. "But don't you want things better for your family? Wouldn't you like some real money and not just the company script?"

"Script is good at the store. I can get everything I need there. You go stirring up a hornet's nest, and we all get stung."

"But don't you want more? If the workers all band together, things can get better for everyone."

"You go in spouting off all that is wrong and things could get a whole lot worse. I seen it at another camp I worked at before coming here. This is downright paradise compared to that place." Marcus held up his hands. "I don't want no part of whatever you got planned." He strode away.

Lindley couldn't understand. Marcus didn't even want to try to make things better. Did all the men feel the same way?

Marcus was one of the biggest men in camp and an undeclared leader among the miners and kiln workers. Everyone looked to him more than the foreman. Without Marcus's support, Lindley could do very little. But he would do what he could.

On the following Monday, three of Bridget's students were home sick with colds, including one of the Bennett children. On Tuesday, two more of the Bennett children were out sick. At lunchtime, Mr. Thompson showed up at the school. Though he looked every bit the miner now, she still wondered about him.

Dora ran to him. "Papa!"

He scooped up his daughter, strode to where Bridget sat on the schoolhouse steps and tipped his hat. "Good afternoon, Miss Greene."

As she moved to stand, he held out his free hand to her. She placed her slender fingers in his and stood. A small thrill danced through her. Wherever this man had come from, he was taught good manners. "Good afternoon, Mr. Thompson."

"I came to ask a favor of you."

"I'll see what I can do."

"Several of the Bennett children are ill. I was wondering if Gabe and Dora might go home with you in the afternoons. Just until I get off work and just until the Bennett children are well. I would see if they could go home with another family, but so many have sick children."

She should say no for many reasons. She didn't want the other students or parents to think she was choosing favorites in her class. She also didn't want people to start whispering that there was something going on between her and Mr. Thompson.

And most of all, she shouldn't get involved with this man. He had secrets. She was sure of it. But when she opened her mouth, all common sense flew out of her head. "I would love to look after them." Maybe Gabe and Dora could stay healthy that way.

Dora clapped.

"I really appreciate this. I'll pay you back somehow."

She didn't know how he would ever be able to on miner's wages. But she liked the idea that he would try. It would mean she would likely see more of him. At least every day when he came to retrieve his children. And then by whatever means he would try to pay her back. It was really no trouble. Gabe and Dora were sweet. She lifted up prayers for a quick recovery of the ill children and that her remaining pupils would stay healthy.

By the time the miners got off work, Bridget had a pork-and-potato stew ready with biscuits and a peach pie for dessert.

Gabe sat by the window, watching. "Here he comes!" The boy jumped off the chair and opened the door before his father could knock.

Mr. Thompson remained on the porch. He opened his

mouth as if to speak but hesitated. His nostrils twitched. He appeared to have gotten a whiff of supper. Then he said, "Come on, Gabe. Dora. Time to go."

He must have a tremendous amount of willpower to turn away from a cooked meal. She knew he had to be hungry after a full day of work.

"Miss Greene made supper." Gabe grabbed his father's sleeve and pulled.

Mr. Thompson stumbled across the threshold and gazed at her. "We don't want to impose on Miss Greene's generosity." His words said one thing and his eyes another.

Bridget smiled at him. "It's no imposition." It had been nice having more than just herself at her supper table the other night.

"Come on, Papa." Gabe pushed his father aside and closed the door.

"If you're sure that it's no trouble." Mr. Thompson's stomach rumbled.

She pretended not to hear it. "I would enjoy the company. It would be much better than eating alone."

Mr. Thompson crossed to the sink, but he appeared to have already washed up. "Sure smells good in here."

So he *had* noticed.

After dessert, Dora jumped up from the table. "Can I show Papa your clock?"

"Dora," Mr. Thompson said sharply. "You didn't ask to be excused."

She huffed a breath and climbed back onto her chair. "May I be 'scused?"

"Thank Miss Greene for supper and dessert."

The girl turned to Bridget. "Thank you for supper and dessert." She twisted back to her father. "May I be 'scused now?"

Mr. Thompson grinned at his daughter. "Yes. Take your plate to the sink."

Bridget could see he loved his children very much.

Dora carefully carried her plate to the counter by the sink and then stood by Bridget's chair. "Can I show Papa your pink clock?"

"I'll get it." It wouldn't be appropriate for him to go into her bedroom. Bridget stood.

Mr. Thompson stood, as well.

Bridget acknowledged his courtesy with a nod before she left the room. She returned a moment later with the ceramic clock in her hands and set it on the table. It sat about fifteen inches high and eight inches wide and had pink and yellow primroses painted on it.

Mr. Thompson's eyes widened as he moved around the table to get a better view. "This is really nice."

"Papa, I want a clock just like this."

"Maybe someday, darling." He picked up his daughter. "Time for us to go."

By Friday, Bridget's class of twenty-two had been re-duced to eight pupils, and the first children who had got-ten sick were reported to have whooping cough. Neither Gabe nor Dora was among the sick. It had been prudent of Mr. Thompson to have arranged for his children to stay with her in the afternoons.

At his knock on her door, Bridget's heart sped up. She willed it to slow down. She couldn't let this man climb into her heart. So why had she started preparing enough supper for four? She told herself she was just lonely, but she knew it was more.

People were really going to start talking if this kept up. If not for Dora and Gabe, she would put an immedi-ate stop to it.

Maybe.

* * *

Miss Greene's door opened to Dora swallowed up in a pink apron with a ruffle around the bottom. "I'm helping make supper!"

Lindley smiled down at his daughter. "I can see that." It was good for her to have someone to teach her, even if only for a short while. And the aroma was marvelous.

He reached out his arms to pick her up. But she lifted the front of the apron off the floor as though it were a ball gown, twirled around and trotted back to the kitchen area. His arms were left hanging in midair. He dropped them and settled his gaze on Miss Greene. "I don't suppose it would do me any good to try to decline a supper invitation." He hoped she wouldn't say yes.

She crossed to the door. "Not in the least."

"I didn't think so." He picked up the five-pound sack of flour he'd set just outside the door. "I can't let you keep feeding us without giving you something in return."

She beamed. "That was very thoughtful. Thank you."

He enjoyed the suppers they shared for more than just the tasty food. He enjoyed her company immensely. He didn't want them to end. Not each evening or into the future.

The next night, he brought two pounds of white sugar. Then brown sugar. Then coffee. Salt pork. Lard.

Chapter 7

When Lindley and his children arrived home after supper that following Thursday, Marcus stood in front of his house. His relationship with the man had been strained since their talk two weeks ago about grievances. And so went the attitudes of the rest of the men. Without Marcus, Lindley had not been able to find out what the men and their families needed changed most. Though he had a good idea from his own recent experiences.

Lindley opened his front door. "Gabe, Dora, go get ready for bed." His children scurried inside. He stayed out. "Is this a social call?"

Marcus rubbed the back of his neck. "Not exactly. Can we talk?"

"Want to come in?" He still hoped to get Marcus on his side.

"Not in front of the children. You go see to them." The big man glanced around. "I'll wait out here."

Lindley nodded and went inside. To say he was surprised by Marcus's visit didn't adequately cover it. The man hadn't spoken more than two words to him in over a week. He hustled his children to bed and went back outside. "All right. What did you want to talk about?"

Marcus hesitated and cleared his throat. "Those grievances you spoke of."

Lindley had figured he would give him another week

before broaching the subject again. "I haven't done any-thing about that yet." He really needed Marcus's support.

"I know." Marcus glanced around again and shifted his bulk. "But I want you to."

Lindley could only stare at the man. Marcus was sud-denly supportive of his position? With no coercing? "You were pretty adamant. What changed your mind?"

"My littlest one, only a year old, has the coughing."

"Marcus, I'm sorry. Did you take him to the doctor?"

"Doc says there ain't much he can do. His resources are for the men, to keep them healthy for working. Hardly glanced at my son."

Lindley's body tensed. "Is your boy real bad?"

"Not yet, but he's not getting better. Decker's six-month-old boy passed just yesterday from the coughing."

Lindley didn't know Decker.

"We have a doctor, but he ain't no help when we need him. Leastways not for our families."

"That's not right." Lindley shook his head. It wasn't likely that he could convince the doctor to treat the child if Marcus couldn't. At least not tonight. "When I was a boy and had a bad cough, my mother used to have me breathe in the steam from the teakettle. She would drape a towel over my head to keep the steam from evaporating. It would make me cough like the dickens, but then I could breathe better for a while."

"Thank you. I'll try that." Marcus turned to walk away and then stopped. "We'll talk about those other grievances tomorrow." He left.

Lindley was sorry for Marcus's child being sick but was glad the man was on his side now.

The following week, Bridget sat at her table with Mr. Thompson and his children. Every evening for two weeks, they had eaten supper together like a family. A closeness she'd never had or felt with her own family. No siblings to share life with. But she'd had a string of nannies to keep her company, some good and some who didn't last a week.

It wasn't until she was fourteen that she had been invited to sit at the supper table with her parents, and even then they hardly acknowledged her presence until she was older. They were busy discussing their interests.

But these meals with Lindley and his children were something altogether different. Gabe and Dora spoke freely at the table, not hushed or glared into silence. Instead, their father smiled at them.

Mr. Thompson glanced at her.

The corners of her mouth automatically pulled up, and she warmed all over. The sudden thought that she didn't want these suppers to end popped into her head. *Oh, my.* It was far too early in their friendship to have such thoughts. Wasn't it?

But there was something intimate about eating together. And they had done it every night for two weeks. And he was so good and kind with his children, giving them respect in the way he spoke to them and corrected them. In time, the threat of illness would pass, and Mr. Thompson wouldn't require her help any longer. She couldn't bear to think of how lonesome it would be at her table when their suppers together came to an end.

"There's still some spice cake." She had not had so many sweets in her life until recently. She made sure she always had something for dessert to make supper last longer. But her corset was getting a bit snug.

Mr. Thompson wiped his mouth with his napkin. "I'm afraid I can't stay."

The children whined. Bridget felt like whining as well but refrained.

Mr. Thompson patted the air with his hand to quiet his children and then spoke to Bridget. "I have a favor to ask of you."

"All right."

"The miners are meeting tonight to discuss better working conditions. With so many of the miners' children still ill, I was wondering…if…" He rubbed a hand across his mouth, looked down and then back up. "…if I might leave Gabe and Dora here with you until it's over."

"Oh, dear, the miners aren't going to strike, are they?"

"I don't think it will come to that."

She hoped not.

"So, then, may they stay with you?" His eyebrows pushed up, and he seemed not to breathe.

That meant she would get to see him later. "Oh, yes. Please do."

Dora cheered.

Mr. Thompson stood and ruffled Dora's hair. "Thank you. I really appreciate this. I shouldn't be more than an hour." He put on his hat and left.

A giddiness like a schoolgirl's rose inside her at getting to see him again later. "Who wants a piece of cake?"

Both children raised their hand as though they were in her classroom.

After dessert, Bridget noticed that the heavy mist from earlier had turned into a steady rain. She went to the window and peered out into the inky blackness.

"Your house doesn't rain," Dora said.

Bridget turned to the girl. "Doesn't what?"

Dora spread out her arms. "Doesn't rain. It's all dry. Ours rains right in our bed. Gabe thought it was me, but it wasn't."

"The roof leaks," Gabe said. "Papa had to move our mattress to the middle of the room. He says the mining company needs to fix it."

Mercy. These poor children and the other miners and their families. No wonder so many of her pupils were sick. She knew the houses for the miners weren't sturdy, but no one should have to live in a house with a leaky roof. She was most fortunate to have the little one-bedroom house she did.

An hour passed, then two. "Where's Papa?" Dora yawned for the seventh time.

Gabe was still trying to hide his tiredness by keeping his mouth almost closed as he struggled against yawns. He was fighting one now and turned away from her so she couldn't see.

"Time for bed."

Dora reached up thin arms, obviously ready to call it a day. Bridget obliged by picking her up.

"I'm not tir—" Gabe's mouth gaped wide, unable to stop the yawn.

Dora laid her head on Bridget's shoulder. "Are you taking us home?"

She couldn't do that. "How about if you sleep here?"

Dora nodded as her mouth stretched wide again.

"Where?" Gabe asked.

"I thought you could sleep on the sofa and Dora in the bedroom." She carried Dora to her room and sat her on the bed. She pulled an extra quilt out of her cedar chest and took two of her shirtwaists out of the wardrobe. "Let me get your brother settled in the other room, and I'll be right back."

Gabe sat slumped against the arm of the sofa but jerked upright when she entered the room. "I'm not tired." He yawned.

"I'm sure you're not." She handed him a shirtwaist to use as a nightshirt. "Change into this while I spread out the quilt on the sofa."

Once the sofa was ready, Gabe climbed between the folded layers. "When's Papa going to be here?"

"Soon." She hoped. She was concerned something might have happened to him.

"I'm gonna stay awake and wait for him." His eyelids drooped.

"You do that." *While you lie right here.* If she told him to go to sleep, he would probably try all the harder to stay awake.

When she returned to the bedroom, Dora still sat on the edge of the bed with her feet dangling and her head down, hunched over. Her slow, steady breathing indicated that she was asleep. How the girl had not tumbled head-first onto the floor was beyond imagination.

Bridget knelt and carefully untied her little shoes and then slipped them off. She exchanged the girl's dress for the shirtwaist and tucked her under the covers. Dora didn't appear to wake up during the whole process.

She slipped out of the room and checked on Gabe. His soft snore proved he was asleep, as well.

She went to the window and peered out again. Rain came straight down. And there still wasn't any sign of Mr. Thompson. She put a log in the fireplace, and the flames jumped to life, licking at it. She added another.

Sitting back in her rocker, she picked up a book. Unable to concentrate, she set it aside and retrieved a quilt block she was piecing from her sewing basket. She could sew and worry at the same time. But that too proved futile. She set the cloth aside and gazed into the fire.

Lord, please keep him safe. She hated to think of these children losing both their parents.

A knock sounded on her door. She startled, jumped up and answered it.

Mr. Thompson stood, dripping on her porch.

"You're safe!"

A smile pulled at his mouth. "Did you think I wasn't?"

"I—I just didn't know. You said an hour. And the rain. Anything could have happened."

"Sorry I'm late. The meeting ran longer than I anticipated."

Remembering the children sleeping, she lowered her voice. "Come in out of the rain."

He shook his head. "I'm a soggy mess. I don't want to dirty your house. I'll just collect my children and not inconvenience you any further."

"They're asleep. I thought they could stay here the night. I can take them to school with me in the morning."

He stared at her a moment before speaking. "I wouldn't want to impose on you."

"It might be difficult to carry them both. They'll be soaked as well before you get home. I would hate for them to get sick over a perceived inconvenience. Which, I assure you, it is not."

He studied her. "I fear I have already taken far too much advantage of your kindness, eating your food and leaving my children in your care after school."

Was he going to turn her down? It was his prerogative. But it really was no inconvenience. The children were already asleep.

"I would appreciate not having to drag them out in this weather. May I see them?"

"Of course. Wait here a moment." She returned quickly with two towels. One she tossed on the floor beside the door, and the other she held out to him.

First, he removed his hat, shook the water off and tossed it to the floor of the porch, then did the same with his jacket. He took the towel and dried his hands and face. "There. I'm not so bad now."

No, he wasn't bad at all. "You can stand on this towel." She pointed to the second cloth on the floor.

He stepped over the threshold and closed the door. "Thank you." He patted the worst of the rain off his pants with the towel he'd used on his face.

She motioned him forward and put her finger to her lips. "Gabe is over here." She led him to the sofa in the sitting area in the corner.

He knelt beside his son and brushed a lock of hair off Gabe's face. The act was so tender and loving. Gabe didn't stir.

Bridget couldn't imagine her father ever doing anything so affectionate. Her parents had never been cruel nor hit her, but they had high expectations. If she didn't want to be reproached or put aside, she had better do as she was told. No love or compassion, just expectations. It wasn't until she'd come to know the Lord that she had felt anything like love. She hadn't known what she had been missing.

This man loved his children deeply. And if he loved them, then maybe he could come to love her.

He stood and gave her an inquiring look to ask where Dora was.

She led him to the bedroom and pushed open the door, staying in the doorway. She never imagined a man in her bedroom. But she knew there was nothing inappropriate or intimate about it. He was simply checking on his daughter.

Dora lay on her back in the bed with her arms spread wide and her mouth hanging open. One arm hung off the bed on the far side.

Mr. Thompson rounded the bed, tucked her little arm under the covers and kissed her forehead. Then he bowed his head and closed his eyes. He was praying for his daughter. That must have been what he had done for Gabe, as well.

How sweet. Tears pricked her eyes.

Careful to keep his boots from thumping, he strode out of the room, and she followed him to the front door. "Thank you for letting them stay here. You're right. It wouldn't be good to take them out in this weather. I can't thank you enough." He looked down at the wood floor. "I've still made a mess."

"It's only water."

"And mud from my boots."

"The floor can be cleaned."

He opened the door, stepped out and then put on his wet coat and hat. "Thank you again." He stepped off the porch into the wet, dark night.

She wished he didn't have to leave. She wished they were a family. But he had to, and they weren't.

She watched long after he'd disappeared. She thought of the boy he'd once been who'd been lost on a stormy night such as this. *Lord, keep him safe.* When she could feel the damp air seeping through her clothes, she shut the door.

How could she have such strong feelings for a man so quickly? How could she not for a man so tenderhearted? She hadn't felt like this about any other man in town who had shown her attention. She was curious to see where their budding friendship led.

And her growing feelings.

She turned out the lamp and blew out the candles, save one that she took into the bedroom with her. She readied herself for bed, blew out that candle and slipped in next to Dora. The little girl must have sensed her presence, for she rolled over and snuggled up to Bridget. She in turn reached an arm around the small form. Content, she let herself imagine what it would be like to have these children as her own.

And, of course, their father.

* * *

Lindley lay on his back awake, listening to the rain on the roof...as well as inside this poor excuse for a house. The meeting had gone well this evening. Some of the miners were skeptical at first, as Marcus had been. They were afraid of losing the jobs they already had.

Miss Greene's question haunted him. *The miners aren't going to strike, are they?*

He would do everything in his power to keep that from happening. Not one of them could afford to go a day without pay.

He rolled onto his side. The rain plunk-plunk-plunked into the three pots. Sleep evaded him. Was it the sound of the rain? No. He closed his eyes and listened. Something was missing. He listened harder.

Gabe and Dora.

He couldn't hear them breathing. His son's ever so soft snore and Dora talking in her sleep. His children weren't here. He didn't like being alone at night when it was raining. It was lonesome. Even having two helpless children nearby was comforting. But they were safe. Safe with Miss Greene.

Bridget. He tried out her name in the empty darkness. "Bridget."

He would like to use her first name but hadn't been invited to. Maybe he would ask if it would be all right. Or maybe he would just use her first name and see how she reacted.

She had cared enough to worry over his safety.

He hadn't wanted to leave her this evening, either time. He was comfortable around her. But also on edge. Though he felt at home with her, he didn't know if she felt the same. He'd meant to ask her several times, but then he'd gotten nervous. If she didn't return his affection and turned him away, he knew it would hurt.

Courting hadn't been like that with Doreen. He'd known they would marry and hadn't had to worry about doing something stupid or wrong. He also hadn't had to wonder if she liked him or even loved him. They would marry regardless of either of their feelings. He had come to love Doreen in a way. But these feelings he had for Bridget were different.

Confounding.

Unsure.

It had been easier knowing Doreen couldn't turn him down or away. She was stuck with him long before they ever married, thanks to their fathers.

But Bridget might not return his affections. He would rather think she did than have his feelings crushed. At least for now.

His children were fortunate to get to stay with her. He knew he spent every night at her supper table, but he wanted more.

So much more.

For now he would settle for spending all afternoon Sunday with her. If she would agree to another picnic.

Chapter 8

The next day while Lindley sat outside eating his lunch, Marcus and the other men talked in hushed tones of their meeting the previous night. In the light of a new day, some of the men were more pleased with the prospect of better conditions and others more fearful of retribution. Lindley would need to tread carefully so no one would be penalized.

"You're awfully quiet, Thompson," Gary Bennett said.

He missed his children. It had been only one night, but he'd felt their absence. He was a sorry sap. "Just listening to you ninnies jabbering."

The men laughed.

"You're not gonna back out on us, are you?" Jonesy asked.

"Of course not. I'm determined to make all our situations better."

When the other men moved to head back to work, Marcus put a hand on Lindley's shoulder. "I wanted to thank you. Between what you recommended and the doc looking at him, my boy is improving."

"I'm glad to hear it."

"If there is anything I can do for you, holler."

Lindley paused. "May I ask you something?"

Marcus furrowed his brow. "Your tone sounds personal."

"No." Only personal for Lindley. "How can you tell if a lady likes you?"

Marcus's face relaxed, and he chuckled. "Oh, the schoolteacher's sweet on you, all right."

Lindley looked at his friend sideways. "How did you know I was talking about Miss Greene?"

Marcus wiggled his fingers next to his big blue eyes. "Moony eyes at her. You wait for her before and after church. And, most days, you talk about her so much, the men are getting tired of it."

He hadn't realized he was doing all that, but it was true. Back in his school days, he had friends who did those very things when they liked a girl. He supposed it was easier to see it in someone else rather than himself. "So how do you know she likes me?"

Marcus wiggled his fingers next to his eyes again. "Moony eyes. Looking for you in church when she's up there playing the pie-an-oh. Feeding you and your children supper every night. And her cheeks flush pink when you smile at her, which you do a lot."

He found himself smiling now. He would have to look for her blush.

After work, Lindley washed up and hurried to Miss Greene's. She opened the door, and her cheeks tinged pink. He'd always thought the color was either natural or that it had been from cooking over a hot stove. But he'd watched as the color bloomed and settled nicely on her face.

Once seated at the table and eating, he wanted to ask if he could address her by her first name. Instead, he cleared his throat.

That was the fourth time Mr. Thompson had cleared his throat. He seemed nervous, the way he was fidgeting. "Is there something wrong with your food?"

"No." He cleared his throat yet again. "So do you have family? I mean, are they on the island? Maybe a brother or sister?"

Family? Bridget's insides fluttered. She took her time in swallowing. She had tried to forget she once had a family. It only made her feel guilty. "No. No one on the island. Just me. No siblings. What about you? Brothers and sisters?" Maybe she could distract him.

"Five sisters and one brother. He's the youngest. My sisters doted on him, so he's quite spoiled."

"All on the islands?"

"All on *this* island."

"Are you the oldest?"

"Rachel's oldest. She's my half sister. She's the one who married a British officer during the Pig War. They have nine children. I'm next oldest. Alice is married with four children. Winnie just got married. Edith is engaged. Priscilla is almost eighteen and has several admiring suitors flitting around her, and Todd is thirteen."

Success. He'd forgotten all about inquiring after her relations.

So many siblings and nieces and nephews. He spoke about them with warmth and a smile.

She longed for that kind of closeness. She had left her family behind and now had only herself.

After dessert, Mr. Thompson made his way to the door with his children. "Thank you for another delicious supper."

"You're most welcome." She had been an atrocious cook when she'd first arrived in Roche Harbor three years ago. But she had been determined to feed herself edible meals, so she had pored over cookbooks. Though much improved, she still had a lot to learn. With Mr. Thompson and his children dining with her each evening, she prepared only tried-and-true recipes.

Gabe and Dora scampered out onto the porch.

Mr. Thompson hung back and worked the brim of his hat around and around. "I was wondering if I could…I mean…if you'd allow me to…um… Would you like to use my given name? I mean, I'd like it if you used my given name. Lindley." His ears had turned red.

"Lindley, I'd be honored. And you may call me Bridget."

His smile broke wide, and he tipped his hat. "Good evening, Bridget. Thank you again. And I'll see you tomorrow."

Things were progressing quite well with Mr. Thom— Lindley.

Lindley turned to leave Bridget's porch, but only Gabe stood next to him. "Where's your sister?"

Gabe pointed through the doorway.

Dora stood by the table.

Lindley held out a hand. "Come on."

His daughter shook her head. "I wanna stay at Teacher's house again. She has a soft bed."

Lindley couldn't believe his daughter's boldness. He stepped forward with one foot inside and the other still out. "You can't. Now come along."

Dora grabbed his hand and pulled to keep him in the house. "You can stay, too."

He couldn't believe Dora said that and jerked his gaze to Bridget. Her cheeks were a pretty shade of pink, and she avoided eye contact. He picked up his daughter. "Time to go." He would have to have a little talk with Dora about appropriate and inappropriate things to say. "We'll see you tomorrow."

"Good evening," Miss Greene said as he stepped off the porch.

On the walk home, Lindley's thoughts remained on Miss Gree— No, he could call her Bridget now.

Dora shifted in his arms. "Why didn't you want to stay at Teacher's?"

"It's not that I didn't want to—I mean, I didn't…" He took an exasperated breath. "Dora, you can't invite yourself to stay at someone else's house."

"Why not? We stayed before. And you didn't get to. You would have liked it. Her bed—"

"Dora. Stop." He would push that thought right out of his mind. How to explain it to a four-year-old? "Darling, I can't stay at Miss Greene's house. It wouldn't be right."

"Why not?"

He took a deep breath. "Well, we aren't married. A man and woman can't live in the same house if they aren't married, unless they are already family."

"Then we need to marry her."

We? She obviously didn't understand the concept of marriage. "A man and woman need to be in love before they get married." Even though he hadn't been in love with Doreen. Not really.

"Don't you love her, Papa?"

"Well, I don't know. I haven't known her very long." But he knew his feelings were rapidly heading that way.

Dora wiggled, and he had to tighten his hold so she didn't fall. "Why not, Papa? Why not? You should love her!"

Gabe breathed hard. "She's never going to understand."

Lindley didn't think his son really grasped the concept either, but Gabe liked to act as though he knew more than he really did. "It's not that simple. She would have to love me, too."

Dora patted his chest. "I'll ask Teacher at school tomorrow to love you and marry you."

"No!" He took a deep breath to calm himself. "Dora, you are not to say one word to Miss Greene about love or marriage or staying at her house. Do you understand?"

"But why? Don't you want to marry her?"

Gabe shook his head. "See."

Lindley hung his head. "Honestly, I don't know. But you can't say anything to her. It—it…it might…make her feel bad, and then she might not want us to come over. Promise you won't say anything to her, or I won't let you go to school anymore."

Dora huffed. "I promise. But you should love her."

He just knew his daughter was going to get him in trouble with Bridget. "Gabe?"

"I'm not going to say anything like that."

Good.

"Papa?" Gabe kicked a rock on the path. "Why did you talk like that to Miss Greene?"

"Like what?" He didn't know what his son was referring to.

"All jerky."

Ah, yes. Just before they left. Lindley had sounded like such a fool, trying to ask to use her first name. Fortunately, after he'd made a blundering idiot of himself and still not asked, she had graciously offered him the use of her first name. "I was thinking of other things. I wasn't concentrating. Which is something *you* should never do."

"Can we call Miss Greene Bridget, too?"

"No. She's your teacher. You must always address her as Miss Greene. Do you understand?"

Gabe nodded as he kicked another rock.

Lindley spoke to his daughter. "Dora?"

"What, Papa?"

Did his daughter not hear and understand? Or had she already learned the feminine art of being coy? "You understand that you must continue to call Miss Greene Miss Greene?"

"But if she says I can call her Bridget, can I? Bridget is a pretty name."

"No. Not without asking me first." It wouldn't be proper for his children to accidentally call her Bridget in school.

Dora's words echoed in his head. *Don't you want to marry her? You should love her!*

Bridget was definitely a woman he could see himself falling in love with. But how would he know if he was or not? He definitely couldn't ask her to marry him if he couldn't even ask to address her by her first name.

Chapter 9

Lindley offered Marcus the chair adjacent to Mr. Keen's desk.

The big man shook his head. "I'd rather stand." He leaned against the interior door frame.

Was he hoping to make a quick escape if things turned unfavorable?

The mine manager sat behind his desk, with one elbow on a stack of papers, the other on a flat piece of limestone. His sour expression and narrowed eyes told Lindley the man was annoyed with them for interrupting his day. It wouldn't be prudent to try to cajole Marcus into sitting. The manager would rather they just leave.

Lindley wasn't inclined to comply, so he lowered himself into the chair to let Mr. Keen know they weren't going anywhere. "Marcus and I represent the miners and kiln workers."

Mr. Keen rolled his eyes and sat back, causing his chair to creak. "Thompson, I knew you were going to be trouble the minute I laid eyes on you."

"We aren't here to cause trouble, just want what's fair."

"I don't suppose I can just say no, and the two of you will walk out of here?" Mr. Keen waved his hand toward the door.

"No, sir."

The manager huffed a breath. "Out with it, so I can say no and you two will leave."

Lindley hoped it wouldn't be so. The miners and kiln workers deserved better. "We have six items on our list." He unfolded the piece of paper he held, though he doubted he would need it.

"You're a bit big for your britches expecting so much."

"You're a reasonable man. I'm sure you'll see the merit in what we're asking for."

"I'm sure higher wages is on that list of yours. Always is. We pay what all the other mines are paying. The investors aren't going to agree to an increase."

Lindley expected argument on the wages, but he would still try. "We'll get to wages. It's number three. First, the houses the mine company provides. They are in need of repairs. My roof leaks in three places when it rains. It's a wonder everyone isn't sick. The men will work harder, knowing their families are in safe, warm homes."

Mr. Keen pinched his eyebrows together. "Leaks?"

"Yes, sir. And drafts come in through cracks in the walls. I can see where the previous tenant stuffed paper in mine, but they get wet when it rains and fall out."

Mr. Keen stared at Lindley for a long time without speaking.

Lindley would wait him out, daring him to refuse to repair the houses.

Mr. Keen's gaze shifted up to Marcus. "Your house leak?"

Marcus cleared his throat. "Not mine personally, but I know of several that do."

"Roughly how many?"

"I'd say at least half if not more."

"Make me a list of the houses and what needs fixing

and what supplies will be needed. If I get the materials, will the men fix their own houses?"

"Yes, sir," Marcus said.

"Then I'll see what I can do."

The men shouldn't have to fix company houses without compensation, but it was better than nothing. And the men would be eager to do their own repairs if it meant better living conditions.

"Second, the miners can see the company doctor, but their families can't. Marcus's boy was real sick, and the doctor wouldn't look at him at first. If—"

Mr. Keen held out his hand to stop Lindley. "Doc's first priority is the workers."

"Yes, but—"

"If he has time, the families can see him, but the workers come first. I'll talk to him." Then he quickly added, "But if the families abuse the privilege, it'll be taken away."

Lindley was pleased with that. "Third, wages."

"We already covered that."

"If the men made a little more, they would work harder, and the company could be choosier in whom they hire because everyone would want to work here."

The manager shook his head. "I'll bring it up to the investors, but I know they won't agree to it. Next."

Lindley supposed he couldn't ask for more. "Fourth, script. We want part of our pay in real money."

"No. That won't happen. Next."

"But—"

Mr. Keen leaned forward. "Next." His tone left no room for argument.

Lindley consulted his list even though he didn't need to. Should he try to push for real money? Maybe next time. "Shorter workday. The men would have more energy to work if they weren't so tired."

"Now you're just getting whiny. You sound like an old woman." Mr. Keen waved his hand in Lindley and Marcus's direction. "Lunch break's almost over. Go."

Behind Lindley, Marcus opened the door. His boots thumped against the floor as he left.

Lindley remained seated. "We have one more item—"

"I said, you're done."

Arguing seemed to be futile at this point. Lindley rose slowly, folding his piece of paper and placing it on the desk in front of Mr. Keen. "The men deserve all of these."

"You know as well as I do that the investors will decide."

Lindley would like to put the investors in these men's living and working conditions and see if they didn't want better. He left.

Marcus waited outside and slapped Lindley on the back as he exited. "I'd say that was mighty successful."

Successful? A start, maybe, but not nearly enough.

The men crowded around the pair.

"How did it go?"

"We still got jobs?"

Marcus held up his hands to quiet the men. "Of course you still have your job. And more. Our houses will get fixed and our families can see the doctor."

The men cheered.

But they were still working long days for little money. Script no less. It would have to do for now.

The next few weeks of school went like the previous week. Bridget's eight students had dwindled to six, then after a week picked back up, gaining a pupil or two a day. Dora and Gabe were spared the whooping cough, and for that she was grateful. Two infants in the mining camp had succumbed to the illness. Many of the adults had also become sick. For a while, it seemed as though the whole town was coughing.

The weather had warmed, and school was almost over for the summer. With only a little more than two weeks left, most of her students had returned. At this juncture, there wasn't much point in having Gabe and Dora resume walking home with the Bennetts, who still had an ill child.

On Monday after supper, Lindley followed Bridget to the sink with dirty dishes from the table. His words came out in a rush. "Would you go to supper with me?"

"What?"

"I want to take you to the Hotel de Haro's dining room. I hear they have excellent food."

"I don't know." She couldn't allow him to spend what little money he had. On *her* no less. She glanced back at his children, still seated at her table.

"Just the two of us." His eyes were wide with expectation. "I'll get someone to look after Gabe and Dora."

He wanted to be alone with her? Her heart did a little dance.

This was harder than Lindley ever imagined. His insides felt like a knotted rope. He'd wanted some time with just Bridget but had never been able to muster the courage. He'd been spared all this courting nonsense with Doreen. His father had made an agreement with her father after Lindley had rescued Doreen from a racing freight wagon. He'd known since he was twelve whom he would marry. No falling in love or worrying about whether she loved him. No need to get nervous. They were betrothed, and that was the end of it.

Doing this on his own was different. Hard.

He wiped his sweaty palms on his trousers. What if she turned him down? He'd waited long enough so that he was fairly certain she cared about him and not just for his children. Looks she gave him. The blush in her cheeks when he caught her staring. Always having supper ready.

Her silence unnerved him. "I mean, it *is* the least I can do after all the meals you have provided for me and my children." There. Now she might feel as though she could accept because it didn't sound so much as if he was trying to court her. Which he was.

But was he really in a position to be courting this fine lady? That didn't seem to matter. The more she hesitated, the more he wanted her to say yes. Once alone with her, he could make his intentions known.

She looked down. "Lindley, the hotel dining room is… expensive."

Was she embarrassed?

She continued. "I know miners don't make much. I would feel bad if you spent your money on me."

"So, your hesitance is the cost and not me?" Relief hovered over him in anticipation.

"Of course."

He let out his breath. This from a woman with a very expensive clock. "So if I were to invite you to…let's say… go for a walk with me, you might accept?"

Her cheeks tinged pink. "Of course. That would be lovely."

"Then I invite you to take a walk with me on Saturday to the Hotel de Haro's dining room. Don't worry about the money. I have a little tucked away. I really want to take you there. Please."

She was silent again. And just when he thought she was going to turn him down, she said, "I'd like that." And the pink of her cheeks deepened.

Bridget closed the door and leaned against it after Lindley and his children left. She couldn't believe she had said yes. Was she touched in the head?

The man likely didn't have the kind of money needed

for the hotel restaurant. And even if he did, he should save it for his children. But the thought of spending time with just Lindley made her skin tingle with delight.

She pictured herself married to him and the four of them a happy family. Such nonsense. She still couldn't figure the man out. But right now, she didn't care a fiddle about that.

For the rest of the week, her insides were all aflutter. On Friday, he told her he didn't need her to look after Gabe and Dora, that one of his sisters was visiting. She found herself disappointed at that. She would truly miss the children. They had become part of her daily life.

On Saturday afternoon, she decided to purchase some perfume. She hadn't worn any since her arrival in Roche Harbor. Hadn't brought any with her and hadn't felt the desire for any.

Until now.

Maybe a rosewater or lilac. She would have to see what her choices were.

Oh, she knew she was being silly but didn't care. Lindley obviously liked her, so a little perfume wouldn't make him like her more. But she wanted supper to be special.

She entered the general store run by the mining company. The scents of sweet lavender soap, pungent kerosene and tangy dill pickles assailed her nose. The perfumes were tucked under the counter, and Mr. Miller was attending to a customer already. So she strolled around the store. Candles. Matches. Pots and pans. Books. Bolts of yard goods.

Glancing up, she gazed through the large plate-glass window. A man in a sharp suit, who resembled Lindley in height and build, stood across the street. She moved closer to the pane of glass but, from this angle, could see more of his back than anything. Under a low flat-top derby hat, his hair was neatly combed down. He spoke with the mine manager and another gentleman. All three men were dressed in fine suits.

The one who reminded her of Lindley turned, and she could see him better.

Lindley?

She gasped and stepped back from the window, bumping into a display. A tray of sewing notions tumbled to the floor. Spools of thread thudded as they bounced and rolled. Thimbles scattered and skittered beneath a shelf.

Mr. Miller gazed over at her, squinting his eyes.

"I'm sorry. I'll clean this up." She squatted and gathered spools, thimbles and packets of needles off the dusty floor and put them all back in the tray. She was hidden below the windowpane but couldn't stay there.

Slowly, she rose, staring out the window.

Lindley and the two men still stood across the street, talking. The third man made her think of a Pinkerton detective she had once met. She gasped again. He wasn't here for her, was he? She stepped back from the window. She couldn't let him see her. Any of them.

What was Lindley doing in a suit and talking to those men?

Who was he?

Obviously not a miner. Not in those clothes. Was he a Pinkerton, as well? The thought stabbed her in the chest, and she caught her breath.

She had known from the start that he didn't seem like a miner, and now she knew why. He wasn't. Had he been trying to trick her all along?

She waited until Lindley and the men left and moved toward the door.

"I appreciate you picking those up for me." Mr. Miller nodded to her. "Can I help you?"

"N-no, thank you."

"You came in for something."

"No. No. I'm fine." She hurried out the door and closed it. Glancing both ways, she crossed the street, her pace *very* unladylike. She peeked over her shoulder every few seconds until she reached her little house and entered.

She turned the lock on the door and heaved several breaths. She had been foolish to think she wouldn't be found out. After three years, she had become complacent, thinking a strip of water would keep her hidden. She pulled back her pink gingham curtain, peered out, but saw no one.

What should she do?

She strode to her bedroom and then back out to the front window. Her shoes beat heavily on the wooden floor as she moved from one room to the other and back. Stopping, she glared at her feet. Someone might hear her. That was silly. Just the same, she walked on the balls of her feet, making as little noise as possible.

Finally, she sat on the edge of her bed and buried her face in her hands. How could she have been so foolish? As she had suspected, Lindley Thompson was no miner. How could she let herself fall in love with him?

It was simple. She would leave. She opened her trunk and tossed in two of her dresses. She wrapped her French clock in one of her petticoats. When the trunk was nearly full of her belongings, she stared at it. She couldn't haul the trunk. Not if she left in a hurry. The carpetbag. She would be able to carry the carpetbag. She plopped it on the bed and sorted through the trunk, figuring out what to pack.

Why had he waited so long? Two months? If he knew who she was, why wait?

What about her students? She couldn't leave them before the end of the term. If Lindley had waited this long, maybe he would wait until school was out. But could she risk it?

She pictured each of her students. Every one eager to learn. Daniel, Suzanne, Faye, Jill, James, Aggie, Carol, Donita, Heidi...Troy. If she left, he would have no chance at a better life. None of them would.

Regardless of the risk to her, she would stay until the end of school and slip away during the night.

If Mr. Thompson tried to take her away before then, she would appeal to his better nature to let her finish the school year. She would even use his children against him as he had used them to gain her trust. Were they even his children?

She wanted to back out of supper but didn't know how without making him suspicious. Maybe this evening was when he would tell her she had been caught.

Her heart ached that he was not who he said he was. She tried to muster anger at him for lying, but her fear kept it at bay.

Lord, please let me be wrong about him being a Pinkerton. Let him be the simple miner I've come to care for. Come to love.

Her heart refused to see anything except the simple miner and loving father. But her head screamed for her to run, that he had tricked and manipulated her.

And threatened her very existence.

Chapter 10

Two hours later, when the knock came on Bridget's door, she jumped, unsure if she should answer it. Pretend she wasn't home? Or go to her doom? And so had gone the afternoon, back and forth. Heart or head? Head or heart? But, in the end, her heart needed to know who he really was. *And* if he was going to betray her or not.

Taking a deep breath, she smoothed her dress, prayed he was in his miner's clothes and opened the door.

Her heart plummeted like a ship pitching in a stormy sea. His fancy suit from earlier. He could have gotten it from a missionary barrel like his children's Sunday clothes.

She forced a smile. "My, don't you look dapper."

He stared at her a moment. "And you look lovely. Are you ready?"

She pulled a shawl from the peg by the door and wrapped it around her shoulders. She was cold, even though the day had been warm. "Yes."

"The hotel's not far. I hope you don't mind the walk."

"A walk will be lovely." She preferred walking anyway. If he was indeed a miner, all his money was going to pay for supper. If he had rented a buggy, she would have known for sure he wasn't who he claimed to be. She took his offered arm and did her best to keep up her end of the commonplace conversation.

She had forgotten how lavish the hotel and dining room were. Candlelit chandeliers flickered light and shadows around the room, taunting her. White linen adorned the tables with silver, crystal and china upon them.

Lindley couldn't afford this. She was about to say so when a waiter in a crisp white shirt and black bow tie greeted them and deftly led the way across the room. He stopped at a table by a window that overlooked the harbor. She sat and gratefully accepted the offered menu, something to hide behind and focus on. She didn't want to see betrayal in Lindley's eyes.

Once she ordered and no longer had the menu to occupy her, she straightened her silverware, making them all even, and smoothed her napkin, centering it exactly square on her lap. "This is a very nice place."

"Have you eaten here before?"

"Once, more than a year ago." She felt him staring at her but didn't dare to look up.

"Is everything all right?"

Her emotions were in such a tangle she was sure tears would burst out of her at any moment. She would not fall apart. She had been trained better than that. "Yes, I'm fine." Please let him be everything she thought he was before. Miner, father, friend. "You look… I mean your suit… Where…? Um…it's very nice."

He tugged on the lapels of his jacket. "Do I tidy up all right?"

"Oh my, yes." But where had he gotten the fine clothes? Please let it have been a missionary barrel.

"You look fetching yourself. Is that dress new?"

The pink silk had a wide neckline with lace and intricately folded fabric down the front of the skirt. "No. I just don't get much opportunity to wear it. It's not appropriate for the schoolroom." And several years out of fashion.

"It's quite fancy."

Oh, dear, he knew. She shouldn't have worn this dress. She should have chosen something more ordinary. If tonight was to be special, as she originally thought, she had wanted to look her best.

When the food arrived, the nausea Bridget had kept at bay rolled inside her. She was going to be ill if she didn't distract herself.

Lindley bowed his head and said a prayer over their food. Right there in public. He even prayed for the evening to go well.

She hoped it went well too as she picked at her salmon, taking the smallest of bites.

"Is your meal all right?" He pointed with his fork.

"Oh, yes, it's fine."

"You don't seem to be eating."

Trying to act normal obviously wasn't working. "I don't have much of an appetite, I guess."

"Bridget." He set his fork down. "I'm afraid I have misjudged things."

"How so?"

"I had hoped this evening would be the start of something between us." He gently laid his hand on hers resting upon the table. "But you seem nervous to be alone with me."

She fought the urge to jerk free out of self-preservation. But at the same time, she relished his warm touch.

He slipped his hand under hers and gently held it. "I like you. Very much."

And she liked him. She raised her gaze to him for the first time that evening.

Earnestness embedded in his eyes. "I thought—or rather, hoped—you felt the same. If I was mistaken, I'm truly sorry." He didn't sound like a Pinkerton.

Her apprehension fell away. "You weren't mistaken." *Please don't break my heart.*

The corners of his lips curved up. "There's something I've been wanting to ask you— No. First, there's something I must tell you. I'm not really a miner."

Her breath froze in her chest. She had surmised that already. *Please, not a Pinkerton either.* She slipped her hand from his and smoothed her napkin. Her words came out in a squeak. "You're not?"

"I work for one of the investors of the mine. My father-in-law. The mine wasn't making the profit that the numbers said it should. He wanted me to find out if there was a more efficient way of running the operation. If the workers were stealing and things like that."

She stared at him, turning his words over in her mind. Not a Pinkerton. "So that really is your suit." What an idiotic comment.

He furrowed his brow. "Whose else would it be?"

"A real miner wouldn't be able to afford such a suit." His confession solidified in her brain. He had been pretending to be someone he was not. "But since you are not a *real* miner, you *obviously* can." Anger rose inside her. "I felt *sorry* for you *and* your children. I know how hard it is for the miners to feed their families, and you with no garden to help put food on the table. You really *can* afford to eat here, can't you?"

"I thought that would be good news. I have no problem providing for myself and my children."

No wonder he'd *hired* someone to look after Dora when he'd first arrived. He *had* the money to. But he must have thought better of it when he realized he shouldn't be able to afford it.

"I feel like such a fool. Quite gullible, I am. Tell me anything, and I'll believe it." On the verge of tears, she blinked rapidly but from shame rather than fear this time. This was nothing to cry about. He wasn't a Pinkerton. Fear, anger, shame, relief and a dozen other emotions tumbled around inside her.

"I'm sorry for misleading you. I had a duty and a job to fulfill. I had hoped you would understand." His eyes pleaded.

Understand? Yes, she understood. Better than most. He was *not* a Pinkerton come to drag her back. The realization wrapped around her like a warm quilt. She was not at risk.

Mirth bubbled up inside her.

He had been brave enough to confess and trust her. Should she, as well?

Her mother had taught her not to diminish a man by turning the focus from him. Let him have his moment and find another time to reciprocate if need be.

She didn't want to spoil the evening with another confession. One was certainly enough.

Maybe tomorrow after church.

Finally, a smile.

Lindley breathed a little easier with the weight of his pretense lifted. Tension seemed to drain from her whole demeanor, releasing her. He allowed himself to relax a little, as well. But she still hadn't said anything.

He had worked his insides into knots with worry over how she would react. And from the time he'd arrived at her home until now, she'd seemed nervous and aloof. Before he'd even confessed. Maybe she had sensed something was amiss from the start.

He'd wanted to tell her sooner but didn't know how and was afraid it would affect his job and others would discover his purpose. He had been ordered to tell no one. Only Mr.

Keen had known his true intentions in being at the mine. "Please say you understand."

Finally, she spoke. "I admit that I was a bit taken aback, but I do understand. I mean, you were working for the mining company, in a sense. Just in a different capacity." She took a sizable bite of her salmon.

"Yes, I was."

She swallowed. "You never quite seemed like the other miners."

So she *had* noticed. "I didn't? What gave me away?"

"For starters, your clothes." She took another bite.

Pleased to see her finally eating, he said, "I bought the same clothes as the other miners wore. I even made them dirty so they would appear worn."

"Yes. But they still looked new. And the dirt on both you and your children didn't seem natural. I asked myself why you would purposefully sully your clothes. I could never figure it out."

He had wrongly assumed that dirty was dirty. "So, what else?"

"Your hands."

He turned his hands over. They were calloused from the past two months of physical work. Traces of mine dust and grime were still embedded under his nails.

"When you first arrived, they didn't look as though they had seen a hard day's work. Unlike now."

"Oh, they have seen plenty of hard work, just not in recent years. It actually felt good to do physical labor again. There is something quite satisfying about it. Anything else?"

"Your diction."

He raised his eyebrows.

"Your manner of speech, and you used words the average miner would not. Then there was your concern for

Gabe's grades. Though a lot of the miners are grateful their children can get more schooling than themselves, they don't value it. They know their sons and daughters will end up doing the jobs they do and wouldn't use an education."

He shook his head. "And here I thought I was doing so well at blending in."

She actually gave a small laugh at that. And before long, she had eaten all her supper.

He was glad to see that her appetite had returned. Now maybe the evening wouldn't be a loss.

Bridget had savored every bite of her meal, relieved Lindley wasn't a Pinkerton come to take her home. On the morrow, she would disclose her own pretense, though nothing as elaborate as his.

After supper, he escorted her down by the harbor and to the end of the dock, where waves gently lapped at its pillars. Moonlight danced on the water's surface. A gentle breeze carried in the salty air.

A perfect evening.

Lindley shifted his position. "The mining-company investors are hosting a party next Saturday. Businessmen and other potential investors from across the islands and the mainland will be here. I would very much like you to accompany me."

Mainland? "You don't want me at some fancy party." In fact, she couldn't go. It would be most unwise.

Facing her, he took her hand. "I *want* you at my side."

She didn't miss the deeper meaning to his earnest words. She *very much* wanted to be at his side. But if the wrong person saw her, the past three years would have all been for naught. "I don't have an appropriate dress for such an occasion."

He held out her arm and glanced down her dress. "This will do just fine."

That was kind of him, but she knew better. This dress would pale in comparison with the gowns of the other ladies who would likely be in attendance. But it would be plenty fancy for a schoolteacher.

"Please?" He squeezed her hand in both of his.

She should say no.

But she wanted to go.

But it was unwise.

But her heart cared naught for wisdom.

Careful, her head cautioned.

She held a great deal of fondness for Lindley and his children. Enough to risk everything? What were the chances that there would be anyone attending who would know her or recognize her? "Very well. I'd love to go." Her heart won out over good sense. She was both thrilled and terrified.

"Thank you." He pressed his lips to her hand, causing a tingle to radiate up her arm and through her body.

And she knew she was in love. She would risk most anything for him.

He tucked her arm around his and walked her home.

As she turned to retreat inside, Lindley touched Bridget's arm to stay her.

She gazed up at him.

"Tonight I was hoping to ask you— Well, I wanted to ask long before tonight." He took a deep breath. "May I court you?" There, he'd said it. And now his heart thundered so hard in his chest it hurt, and he was sure she could hear it.

She smiled demurely. "I would like that very much."

"You would?" That was the answer he had wanted, but he still couldn't believe it.

"Yes, I would. I do have one more week of school. It would be best to wait until it's concluded." She gazed up at him.

He caressed her cheek with his fingers. The emotions he'd held at bay broke free, knowing she felt the same. Her skin felt like silk under his touch.

Her tongue flicked across her pink lips.

They seemed to invite him closer. Cupping her face, he stepped forward.

She didn't pull back or turn away from him.

He pressed his lips to hers. Warm and inviting. Slightest pressure.

She wrapped her arms around his waist.

He intensified the kiss.

After several moments, he broke off but kept his mouth very close to hers. "I guess this means we didn't wait for school to be out, Miss Greene."

"Apparently not, Mr. Thompson." Smiling, she slipped inside her house.

Curious that he wasn't nearly so nervous with her now. He supposed having kissed her and she kissing him back would do that. He looked forward to the next time.

His mouth hitched up on one side as he backed off her porch to head for home.

Bridget leaned against her door, listening to Lindley's footsteps descending her porch and crunching on the dirt. She rushed to the window and could see him in the moonlight. He appeared to have a spring in his step. She sighed.

All that worrying for naught. He had been harboring a secret, but not one that concerned her. At least not directly. And now she was being courted by a man she loved with her whole heart. A man she had pictured herself married to.

A man who deserved to know *her* secret, as well.

She pushed the thought aside. Certainly he would be as understanding.

She must go unpack.

Chapter 11

It warmed Bridget's heart to see the church full once more with everyone well again. When she finished the final hymn and turned from the piano, she looked for Lindley at the back. She halted, perched on the edge of the piano bench, and stared.

Three young ladies and a young man stood with him and his children. None of whom she had ever seen before. And all were gazing at her with smiles. One lady held Dora, and the man held Gabe. She hadn't realized the new people were with Lindley.

He'd said his sister was in town. But that would account for only one of them and not the man.

She stood.

Lindley left the gaggle and met her at the first pew. "Evidently, Priscilla telegrammed my family about you, and they sent a scouting party. They arrived last night while we were at supper."

She picked up her black leather-bound Bible and tucked it in the crook of her arm. "Are they all your siblings?"

"Just the girls. Emmett is married to Winnie. They couldn't come without a chaperone."

"Half your family came?"

"Oh, this isn't even half of them with all the nephews and nieces. Come, and I'll introduce you."

"I…" She shifted her Bible. They would be a lot to take in all at once. And he had more family elsewhere on the island. A lot more.

"My sisters won't relent until they meet you." He picked up her shawl and hat and then led her down the aisle.

Four pairs of expectant eyes stayed fixed on her. Did she look all right? She touched her hair and glanced down. She was glad she had worn her favorite green-and-white-striped spring dress adorned with white lace.

Dora leaned toward her, and Bridget instinctively reached for the girl and settled her on her hip, as naturally as if she were her own.

Lindley took Bridget's Bible and motioned to her. "This is Miss Greene. Bridget, these are three of my sisters. Winnie and her husband, Emmett Halsted. Edith. And Priscilla."

Bridget nodded to each person in turn. "Mr. and Mrs. Halsted, Miss Thompson, Miss Priscilla, I'm very pleased to meet all of you."

Dora piped up. "I'm Dora."

Everyone laughed, and tension rushed out of Bridget.

Mr. Halsted dipped his head toward her. "We are all pleased to meet you, Miss Greene. You may call me Emmett."

The young ladies had eager gazes. Their smiles pressed into thin, upturned lines, as though they wanted to speak but were forcibly keeping their mouths closed. One even appeared to be holding her smile between her teeth. But all three remained silent.

Bridget wondered why. She dipped her head to the man. "Emmett, I'm honored. Please call me Bridget."

"I'm honored."

"Well, you must call me Winnie," the sister who wore a burgundy calico dress said.

"And me Edith." In blue calico.

"Just Cilla for me." Yellow calico.

"I couldn't believe Lindley didn't tell one person in the family about you." Burgundy calico.

"You will have to give us all the details about yourself." Blue calico.

Bridget didn't know which sister to focus on. They practically spoke on top of one another as though a dam had ruptured. And she daren't try to squeeze in a word. There wasn't room.

"You're the schoolteacher." Yellow.

"Dora and Gabe told us all about you." Blue.

"I was a schoolteacher until I married Emmett." Burgundy.

"Have you lived on the island long?" Blue.

Bridget tried to nod, but the next question came too quickly and several more after that.

Lindley held up his hands. "Not all at once."

His sisters apparently hadn't heard him and kept talking.

Emmett shrugged, his gaze on Lindley. "You tried."

Or maybe they were ignoring their brother? Had he told them ahead of time not to deluge her with questions?

"Your dress is lovely," one sister said.

Dora patted Bridget's dress.

"The color of your hair is lovely," another said.

Dora patted Bridget's auburn hair.

"Everything about you is lovely," the third sister said.

Dora squeezed Bridget around her neck. "I love her!"

From his uncle's arms, Gabe stretched out his hand and touched her shoulder. He apparently didn't want to be left out but knew better than to try to talk while his aunts were engaged.

Lindley tried again to quiet his sisters, to no avail. So

he looped Bridget's free arm through his and walked away with her.

"Lindley! What are you doing?" one of his sisters asked.

"Taking Bridget away from you clucking hens."

Winnie scooted around in front of them and blocked their way. "No, you don't." She took Dora from Bridget and handed her to Lindley. Then she wrapped her arm around Bridget's. At the same time, Edith hooked her arm through Bridget's now free one. Cilla pressed in behind them, squeezing out the men and children.

And that was how one disentangled a person from a situation. An expert move. Had they planned that?

The sisters ushered her toward the door.

Bridget glanced back at the men. Lindley stood slack-jawed, and Emmett smiled, shaking his head. Dora and Gabe waved.

"You are coming to dinner."

"We have most of it prepared."

The ladies jostled around to all get out the door. Not one of them looked back to see if the men and children were coming.

"We made a pie and a cake and cookies last night."

"We didn't know what you preferred."

Bridget couldn't keep up with who was saying what. "Dinner?"

"Yes. At Lindley's."

"I hope you like chocolate."

"We'll have it ready in a trice."

"And peach."

"You won't have to do a thing."

"But his place…" She couldn't imagine how his small house could accommodate all these people. And with the roof leaking. "Will we all fit?" Even her house would be stretched with them all.

"Of course."

Bridget glanced at the darkening clouds. "But it looks like rain."

Cilla giggled, much like Dora. "What does that have to do with you coming to dinner?"

Edith looped her arm through Bridget's. "Then we better hurry before the clouds burst."

The sisters hustled her down a road away from the mining camp. She wanted to correct their direction, but they were busy discussing what needed to be done first upon arriving. They would soon realize their error and turn around.

Instead, they ushered her up the path of a quaint, yellow cottage with white shutters. Bigger than her own. Bright pink rhododendron bushes stood sentry alongside the walk, and large lilacs guarded at the corners of the house.

"What? Who?"

Gabe and Dora ran ahead to the door.

Lindley came up as close to her as he could with his sisters gathered around. "We've moved."

That made sense. Since he wasn't a miner, he wouldn't stay in a company house. His change in status was going to take some getting used to. "This is nice."

"Gabe and Dora are excited to each have their own room. We have a kitchen and separate sitting room. Much better than the company houses. But they are going to be repaired."

Edith squealed. "I just got hit by a raindrop. Hurry inside." She ran up the walk and through the doorway.

A drop hit the side of Bridget's nose and another on her hand. Then they splatted here, there and everywhere.

Everyone ran for cover. Lindley ushered her in, his limp more pronounced.

The house smelled of fresh bread, stew and sweets. Though cozy, everyone fit comfortably.

Dora held out her arms. "No rain."

"What does that mean?" Winnie asked. "It went from dry to pouring out there in a matter of a couple of seconds. There's plenty of rain."

Gabe spoke up. "Our other house leaked."

Winnie jerked her gaze to Lindley.

He cringed and shrugged. "It wasn't that bad. We were always dry and warm. I made sure of it."

"I'm hungry," Emmett said. "When's dinner going to be ready?" Kind of him to distract the sisters.

Lindley gave his brother-in-law a nod of appreciation.

The ladies shooed the men and children out of the kitchen and scurried around.

Bridget stood near the door. "What can I do to help?"

All three sisters shook their heads, but Edith spoke. "Oh, you get comfortable, and let us do the work."

That wouldn't be right. "I can't sit idly while you all bustle around doing the work."

Winnie came over and gave her a hug. "I love you for that. You can slice the bread."

The meal was delicious, and the afternoon flew by.

Father and uncle carried the sleeping children to their rooms.

When Lindley returned, he sat next to Bridget on the sofa in the sitting room. "I'm sorry about my sisters."

She'd had a lot of fun with his family. "Don't be." She would have liked to have had a sister or two.

"They haven't scared you off? They can be a bit much."

"Not at all. I like them a lot."

"The rain has let up. Shall I walk you home?"

She was reluctant to leave the camaraderie. But in truth, the three sisters had worn her out more than a classroom full of children. His sisters had welcomed her and treated her like one of them. But the looming clouds wouldn't recess for long.

Lindley retrieved Bridget's Bible, shawl and hat.

"You aren't taking her away from us, are you?" Winnie asked.

"The rain has stopped for the moment. I think this is a prudent time to take her home."

Lindley's sisters each hugged her in turn and told her they adored her. "We hope to see you again soon."

After pinning on her hat and wrapping in her shawl, Bridget stepped outside with Lindley.

He tucked her hand in the crook of his arm. "Honestly, please don't let them scare you. They really are harmless."

"They didn't frighten me in the least. I like your sisters very much. I haven't had so much fun since I was a child."

Bridget saw the tall stacks of the lime kilns keeping watch over the town to the east and remembered her early-morning inference. "How old are boys when they're first sent down into the mine?"

"Too young. Why do you ask?"

"I have a student—well, had a student, Troy Morrison, who had to quit school to work at the mine to help support his family."

"If his family needs the money, he will be working somewhere, whether at the mine or someplace else."

"I know. It's so sad that parents have to choose between schooling for their children and putting food on the table. Troy was supposed to come for tutoring but hasn't. I hope his father isn't preventing him. He probably doesn't think his son needs any more education, but he has so much potential and a desire to learn. He's bright like Gabe. He just needs a chance."

"And what do you want me to do? Talk to his father?"

"That might help. Maybe if there was a requirement at the company that a person had to be of a certain age before being hired."

"I'll put that in my report to the investors. But I don't expect them to care. And even if the mine company didn't let him work for them, he would find other work."

"Oh, I know. Just that you'll try is wonderful. Thank you."

With her house in sight, a drop the size of a half-dollar splatted on the ground in front of her, then two, then five.

Lindley hurried her up onto the safety of her porch a few moments before the clouds released their bounty in a rush.

Oh, dear. What to do now? She couldn't invite Lindley inside her house. That would be inappropriate without a chaperone. And he couldn't walk home in this. He would get soaked, so he'd have to wait until it let up again.

Since they were stuck on her small porch, there was a question she had wanted to ask but hadn't felt it was her place. Now that they were courting, it wouldn't be inappropriate. With the rhythmic drumming of the rain in the background, she asked, "Tell me about your wife."

"Doreen?"

She nodded. She wanted to know a little about the woman she was invariably being compared with.

"She was pretty. I was nineteen and she was seventeen when we married."

Pretty? That was his first thought of his late wife? "Did you love her very much?"

"I suppose."

What kind of answer was that? "You married her. You must have loved her."

"I came to love her…in a way. Our marriage was arranged by our fathers. I knew since I was twelve I would marry her."

She sucked in a breath. "Arranged marriages are archaic and barbaric."

"That's a little drastic. It really wasn't so bad. Doreen was a nice girl. Sweet."

"But you were forced to marry someone you didn't love." A forced marriage for men wasn't so bad. They didn't seem to care about or need love the way women did. Men could do as they pleased and order women about. And women were expected to mutely obey.

Lindley smirked. "I wasn't literally forced, not at gunpoint or anything."

"But you still weren't allowed to marry for love. Didn't you want to?"

He shrugged. "I don't know. It was easier that way. I didn't fret over who I would marry, wonder if a girl liked me or not, or if I'd get my heart broken like so many of my friends. It all worked out. I counted myself fortunate."

"Fortunate?" She couldn't believe his cavalier attitude. "What about her? Did she count herself fortunate? Being forced to marry someone her father told her she must? Maybe *she* wanted to marry for love."

His mouth cocked up on one side.

Did he think this was humorous in some way?

"After we married, Doreen confessed that she was in love with me."

Bridget's breath caught in her throat, and tears burned her eyes. "How heartbreaking. She loved you, and her feelings weren't returned. You probably have no idea how sad that is. Unrequited love."

Lindley had never felt bad about his marriage before. But now he did. He'd never viewed it from Doreen's side of things. He had been selfish to not consider her feelings. "It's not like I mistreated her or anything. We had a good marriage. Arranged marriages don't have to be bad. My parents' marriage was arranged, and they love each other very much." He wanted to convince her it had been all right.

"So have you already found a husband for Dora? A man who doesn't love her? A man who might be cruel to her or ignore her? A man she doesn't want to marry? Would you force her?"

"Arranged marriages don't have to be like that. They can be good." Why were women always so impractical? He didn't like Bridget thinking unfavorably of him. "No. I won't force Dora to marry anyone she doesn't want to. She can marry for love. Are you happy?"

The pained look in her eyes told him she wasn't.

"I saved Doreen from a racing freight wagon when I was twelve. It was coming straight for her. Being deaf, she couldn't hear it or people shouting at her. I didn't think. I just ran and knocked her out of the way."

He rushed on. If he could explain it all, she would understand. "Her father is a wealthy businessman. My father saw an opportunity to better my standard of living, so he leveraged my act of stupidity. She was unharmed but for a few bruises. I wasn't so fortunate—my leg was severely broken by one of the wagon's wheels. Maybe somewhere deep inside, I felt as though they owed me something in exchange for my permanent limp. But I did truly care for Doreen. Who else was going to marry a girl who couldn't hear? Her father probably knew that, too."

She stumbled back against the door. "You're ashamed that your wife was deaf."

"No."

"But you never would have told me, would you?"

"It wasn't important. See, you're all upset over something silly."

"Silly? You think love is silly?"

"Of course not." His stomach hardened. "This is why arranged marriages aren't such a bad thing." She was being unreasonable. He would not be judged unfairly because of actions and decisions that had been out of his control. "Maybe our ancestors had it right by arranging marriages. Fewer hurt feelings. So to save Dora a lot of heartache, maybe I will find a good husband for her."

"Maybe fewer hurt feelings on the part of men, but certainly not women." She yanked her Bible from his grasp, thrust open her door and slammed it behind her.

He didn't try to stop her. How had this blown so out of proportion? His marriage to Doreen had been a good one in spite of how it started. True, he'd never loved Doreen the way he loved Bridget, but he had cared for her, treated her well and been a good husband to her. What more did a woman want?

From the safety of the porch, he stared out at the rain pouring down, making rivulets on the muddy ground.

Bridget's question came back to him. *So have you already found a husband for Dora?* Until today, he hadn't thought about Dora ever getting married. She was his baby girl. But someday…someday she would marry. Would he choose her husband?

No.

He wanted Dora to have love. But could he watch her heart get broken by some careless man? That would break *his* heart. Wasn't that what made arranged marriages so perfect? No one got a broken heart.

And also…no one experienced this joy and happiness and hope for the future he had with Bridget.

Love was the most wonderful feeling…as well as the most painful when Bridget was angry at him.

He wanted Dora to have this elation of love even if it

meant she risked heartbreak. He would not arrange a marriage for his daughter. But neither would he feel guilty for his own arranged marriage. The years had been good, and he had two beautiful children whom he loved dearly.

If she couldn't understand, maybe she wasn't the woman he thought she was.

He stepped off the porch, and the rain soaked him through in less than a minute. He didn't care.

Chapter 12

Though the rain had let up the following morning, clouds still hung heavy in the sky. Lindley walked his children to school. But once the building was in sight, he held back and sent them ahead. He watched from a stand of trees as Gabe and Dora approached the other children.

Bridget stood on the stoop, monitoring her students. She wore a striking blue-and-black-striped dress. Not only did his heart ache emotionally, he had a physical pain in the center of his chest as if someone were squeezing the life out of him. Even breathing hurt.

He hated her being angry at him, but he didn't know how to make her understand. Make her see that there was nothing wrong with his first marriage. He wanted to tell her he was sorry, but he didn't know what he'd done. What was he sorry for? Sorry she was angry at him? Sorry she disagreed with him? Sorry she was unreasonable?

Just sorry.

He wished he'd never brought up his arranged marriage. When Bridget had asked if he loved Doreen, he should have just said yes. Then they never would have disagreed. And she wouldn't have gotten upset at him. And he wouldn't be stumped as to exactly what he needed to apologize for.

If Doreen hadn't taken ill and died, he would have been happy to be married to her the rest of his life. To grow old with her. But now that he knew the joy of love, he realized he had only been content. But content wasn't bad, was it?

Had he been wrong to enter into the marriage?

No.

Regardless of the reasons, he'd wanted to marry Doreen, and she him. Regardless of their fathers arranging it, they had both wanted it. Regardless that the practice was out of date.

Regardless.

Then why did he feel so guilty?

Bridget raised her head, noticed Gabe and Dora, and looked around, presumably for him. Just as her gaze landed on him, he turned and limped toward Mr. Keen's office. Until he knew what to say, he couldn't face her. He would likely only make matters worse.

The mine manager, sitting behind his desk, looked up. "These clothes suit you better. Did you learn all you needed to for the investors?" He stood and thumbed through a stack of papers on a low shelf behind him.

"Not quite. I need to review the ledgers to see if I can find out why the profit margin isn't what they think it should be."

"How far back you planning to look?"

"I don't know. Until I discover the problem. Or if the problem lies in the investors' greed."

As Mr. Keen sat again, he waved his hand toward a shelf across the room. "Last year's ledgers are over there. There's one for accounts receivable and payable. Another for how deep we're excavating, the amount of limestone taken out of the ground and amount of quicklime produced. A third for supplies, workers and miscellaneous."

He lifted papers on his desk and peeked under them. "This year's are someplace on my desk." But after shuffling several piles around, he opened one desk drawer after another. "Or in the desk. And the ledgers for other years are around here someplace."

How could the man ever find anything in this office?

Lindley glanced around. There was no space for him to work or even set up a small table. Papers, books, rock samples, surveying equipment and *stuff* scattered over every surface in the room. Desk, shelves and even the floor. "Could I take the ledgers home to review them?"

"No need, in fact. I'll be gone a few days. Coming back Thursday." He stood and rounded the desk. "Make yourself at home. If you have a mind to straighten anything up, won't bother me. Too much work for just one man." He grabbed a satchel, stuffed in some papers and rocks, and left.

The manager seemed to be in a hurry.

Lindley glanced around at the chaotic disarray. No wonder the accounts were off. Who could keep track of anything in this mess?

Where to start? Excavate for the ledgers and ignore the mess? Or clean up and hope he unearthed everything he needed?

He walked around behind the desk and sat. Even with the ledgers, he wouldn't be able to work at this desk. If he straightened the surface, he could try to ignore the rest of the room.

He made one pile of surveying reports, another of incoming bills, one of orders for quicklime, the company's orders for wood and other supplies, and several other piles. He came up with only one ledger for the current year, accounts receivable and payable. In a "pile" all its own sat the list of grievances he'd written. It had been buried.

The door opened, and Brady walked in. "Oh, sorry. I didn't know no one was in here." He held two large, thin books clutched in his beefy hand.

"Mr. Keen isn't here. Are those company ledgers?"

Brady held them up. "I have to put in figures and such. Part of my job."

Lindley held out his hand. "I'll take them."

Brady hesitated and then handed them over. "You'll tell Keen I brung them back?"

"Of course." He set them with the other one.

The foreman crossed the threshold to leave.

Before he closed the door, Lindley said, "Brady?"

The man turned back.

"The company recently hired a boy named Troy Morrison. You know him?"

Brady nodded. "Tom's boy."

"Send him here straightaway."

Brady frowned. "He's down below."

"Well, bring him up."

Brady huffed a breath and left. The foreman hadn't been happy that Lindley was now over him, and he had to take his orders.

Lindley stepped over clutter. He opened and closed several filing-cabinet drawers until he found empty folders. Grabbing a handful, he put each pile of papers into a folder and stacked them on the corner of the desk. Then he gathered up last year's ledgers from the shelf, dusted off the rock grit and put them under this year's. He would work backward.

He opened the accounts receivable and payable and scanned the headings and down the pages to get a feel for them. He did the same with the other two current ledgers. He stopped partway through the one that recorded supplies and miscellaneous. Flipping pages back and forth, he compared numbers. Though they appeared to be accurate with similar numbers, something seemed wrong, but he couldn't put his finger on it.

He shuffled through the file folders and opened the one

for accounts payable. He flipped through the papers until he found the one he was looking for.

There it was. He thought he'd remembered seeing an invoice for cordwood delivered. The invoice had a larger number than recorded in the ledger. It was off by only a minute amount.

A timid knock sounded on the door.

"Come in."

A tall, gangly boy of fourteen or fifteen entered. All arms and legs protruding from his clothes. "You asked to see me?"

"Troy Morrison?"

"Yes, sir."

"Please have a seat."

Troy twisted his cap in his hands. "I'll stand, thank you."

"How do you like working for the mining company?"

"It's all right. I'm working real hard."

"I'm sure you are. Miss Greene said you were supposed to meet with her to continue your studies."

"I've been meaning to. But I'm so tired after work, I fall dead asleep. Sometimes before I even eat supper."

The poor boy. "What subjects do you like best in school?"

"All of them."

"Which one are you the best at?"

"Numbers. I can figure any equation Miss Greene gives me. I complete my arithmetic exams real fast. I even wait until most of the time is up and then see how fast I can get them done."

Lindley could see why Bridget had compared this boy to Gabe. He could see a bit of his son in Troy's attitude. Both boys did what they could to make the work they were given more challenging. Bridget was right that this boy had a lot of potential. But he wanted to see just how much potential. "Pull up that chair and sit."

Troy looked around and over his shoulder. "Mr. Brady said I was to get back to work as soon as possible if I wanted to keep my job."

"I'll let Mr. Brady know you are here and aren't being indolent—oh, I meant lazy."

"I know what *indolent* means. Miss Greene thinks she's giving me hard words, but I learn them fast."

A lot like Gabe.

He motioned toward a chair. "I want you to look at some numbers for me. Tell me what you see."

Troy shoved his cap in his back pocket and took a seat, scraping the chair legs on the floor.

Lindley turned the ledger to face Troy and set the open file folder next to it.

Troy's gaze shifted back and forth from the ledger page to the invoice. When he spoke, his tone was unsure. "Numbers don't match?"

That was fast. "Are you unsure?"

The boy straightened his shoulders and spoke with more confidence. "No, sir. The numbers on the invoice are more than the numbers in the ledger."

"See if any of the other invoices don't match."

"Is this like a test?"

"More or less."

He held out his hands. "I'll get them all dirty."

The boy was conscientious. That was good. "There's a pump outside. Wash up and come back."

Troy left and returned posthaste with his hands clean, but little else. The dirt started at his wrists and went up his arms. The boy didn't even look at Lindley but went straight to the papers. Within minutes, Troy had sorted the invoices into piles. He flipped the pages of the ledger back and forth, comparing one invoice after another.

Lindley watched in silence.

Eventually, the boy raised his gaze. "There's an error for all the invoices."

"Every one?"

"Yes, sir. Is that right?"

"Show me."

The boy pointed out error after error. Every one of them so small they were easily overlooked.

Were these just simple mistakes? Or was someone adjusting the books for their benefit? If so, who?

A knock on the door.

"Come in."

A miner covered in dirt entered. His shoulders were slumped and his head was down as if he wasn't good enough to be in the office. "I brung my boy his lunch." He held up a pail.

Lindley stood and offered his hand. "You must be Mr. Morrison." He didn't remember meeting the man when he worked a week underground. He must have been on a different crew.

The man stared at his own grimy palm.

Lindley stepped closer, his arm still outstretched. "It's only a little dirt."

Mr. Morrison rubbed his hand vigorously on his dirty trousers and then shook Lindley's hand. "Call me Tom."

"Tom, pleased to meet you."

"Can my boy come back to work now?"

Lindley knew what the man was really asking. "No need to worry. He'll receive his full day's wage for working in here with me today."

Tom blinked in disbelief. "You can do that?"

Lindley nodded. "Troy has been very helpful already."

"All right, then, I'll leave you be." Tom backed out the door.

"Troy, take a break and eat lunch with your father and return here afterward."

"Yes, sir." The boy jumped up and followed his father.

"And, Troy." Lindley pointed to his arms and face. "Finish washing up."

The boy nodded and left.

Maybe helping Troy would make Bridget see him more favorably. Maybe she would forgive him for whatever transgression she thought he'd committed.

After dismissing her pupils, Bridget followed them outside. Though it had rained off and on all day, at present, the clouds only spit out the occasional drop.

She hoped to catch a glimpse of Lindley again. Instead, Cilla came to retrieve his children. Bridget wondered where the rest of the "scouting party" was. His sisters probably didn't want anything to do with Bridget after her fight with Lindley. But to Bridget's surprise, Cilla walked toward her after hugging Gabe and Dora.

Cilla patted the children on the back and said, "Run along and play for a bit, but stay where I can see you."

Bridget eyed the darkening sky. "It looks like it could start raining again any moment. Would you like to come inside?"

Cilla smiled. "We'd like that." She turned to the children. "Inside."

Gabe spun back around. "May we write on the chalkboard?"

"Of course," Bridget said. "Try not to break any chalk."

Gabe and Dora ran inside.

Bridget let Cilla enter ahead of her. "You came alone?"

She stood at the back of the room away from the chalk-board and children.

"The others returned home this morning so Emmett could get to work."

"I see. And you're staying to look after Lindley's children." He probably didn't want Bridget watching them again.

"Yes." Cilla hesitated and then continued. "I don't know what Lindley and you fought about last night, but he is torn up over it. I've never seen him so happy and so devastated all in the span of one day."

Bridget shifted her gaze to the children's chalk drawings. A horse and a scribble. 'Twould be inappropriate to talk about this matter with anyone except Lindley.

"I understand if you don't feel right confiding in me." Cilla adjusted the cuff of her pink shirtwaist. "I just thought you should know Lindley is quite upset."

Though his sister might be able to give her some insight, she shouldn't. "I don't know."

"It's Doreen, isn't it?"

"How did you know?"

"I didn't." Cilla shrugged. "But it was a logical guess. You think he can't love another woman, and he's just after a mother for his children. Well, he's not."

Bridget never thought Lindley was seeking someone to merely care for his children. Cilla had to have been quite young when her brother married. Was she even aware his marriage was arranged? Bridget had best keep that to herself. It wasn't her place to tell Lindley's sister.

"Cilla, you are very sweet to have come, but I don't think I should talk about such things." Now that she thought more closely, this wasn't about Doreen at all, but forced arrangements.

Chalk squeaked on the board, sending a shiver down her spine.

The children laughed and tried to make more squeaks.

Lindley's sister slid into a back-row desk and folded her hands on it, apparently planning to stay awhile. "We can talk about something else." She seemed to just want to visit.

Bridget sat at the desk across the aisle. "Tell me about Winnie and Emmett. Were they very much in love when they married?"

"Oh, yes. But it wasn't always so. Winnie didn't want anything to do with him when he first started coming around. But he was persistent. After two years of Emmett following her around and her ignoring him, Papa finally told her to stop being petty and foolish."

Oh, dear. "He didn't force her to marry him, did he?"

Cilla shook her head. "He told her to give the poor man a chance or cut him free to find someone else. Someone who *deserved* a fine young man like him. I think she was always secretly in love with him. She just wanted to see how deep his devotion was. A week later, they were engaged."

"Would your father ever force any of you to marry someone you didn't want to?" This was treading dangerously close to Lindley's arranged marriage. She hoped Cilla didn't make the connection.

"No. Papa threatens he will, but he won't."

"So if he said you had to marry someone and you said you didn't want to, he wouldn't force you?"

Dora screeched. "Give it back!"

Cilla clapped her hands. "Gabe. Dora. If you two don't behave and play nice, I'll make you sit in a desk." Without missing a beat, Cilla continued the adult conversation.

"No. He really just wants us each to be happy. But if he tried, all I'd have to do is threaten tears, and he'd relent."

Being the youngest girl, her father probably gave in to her far too often.

Though Lindley's marriage was arranged, it sounded as if he could have gotten out of it if he'd wanted to. Did he know that?

His cavalier attitude on the subject stil! vexed her. *It was easier. No worries. No broken hearts. Don't be silly.*

Posh.

He was the silly one.

If he thought forced marriages were reasonable, how could she be sure he truly loved her?

Chapter 13

At noon on Tuesday, Lindley strode toward the area where the men ate lunch when it wasn't raining. Loud voices and boisterous laughter met his ears. As he approached, the men fell silent one by one. No one would raise his gaze to meet Lindley's.

He'd expected as much. They now knew he wasn't really one of them. "Marcus, may I have a word with you?"

The big man froze, no doubt contemplating what he should do. He tossed his boiled egg into his lunch pail and straightened to his full height of six foot four. Toe to toe with Lindley, he glared down. "That's Mr. Cooper to you."

Lindley knew Marcus was trying to intimidate him. It was working, but he mustn't show it. With one word from Marcus, they would all attack him. Both he and Marcus knew that. Lindley also knew that Marcus was a fair man with a caring heart who didn't normally hurt others, but he felt betrayed. "Mr. Cooper, the lumber, shingles, nails and other supplies have arrived for the repair work on the houses."

The minutest shift in Marcus's expression told Lindley that the big man hadn't expected supplies to really be provided.

"I want you to be in charge of seeing that they are distributed to those who need them."

Marcus took a half step back and relaxed his shoulders. "I'll see to it right after work."

"I'd like for you to choose three or four other men to do the work and start straightaway."

The big man's shoulders stiffened again. "There isn't a man here who can afford to lose a day's pay."

Marcus had missed Lindley's meaning. "You and the others will be paid your regular wage to repair the company's houses." He had made sure the men wouldn't have to do the work for free.

Marcus just stared.

So Lindley said, "At the end of the lunch break, come to the office and let me know who will be working on the repairs with you." He walked back to the office, not waiting for an answer.

Before long, he heard a knock on the door. "Come in."

Marcus stepped inside. "I have the men you wanted."

Lindley debated which name to call him. Marcus had told him to refer to him as Mr. Cooper, but it didn't suit the big man. Too formal. His given name was friendlier, but he'd been ordered not to use it. Clearly wanting Lindley to know they were no longer friends. "I'm sorry I couldn't tell you my real reason for being here. But I am going to do what I can to help improve things for you and the other workers. The supplies to repair the houses are only a start."

"We appreciate that."

"Friends, Mr. Cooper?" He held out his hand.

The big man clasped Lindley's hand. "Friends. And call me Marcus."

Lindley smiled. "Very well, Marcus. I had the supply wagons taken to the company houses. They need to be unloaded."

Lindley and Marcus led the small band of men to the

housing. He motioned toward the three freight wagons. "I will leave it to you to decide where to unload."

"The men want to work on their own houses. Would it be all right if we rotate different men working each day?"

"Marcus, I am putting you in charge of this whole project. You run it as you see fit. If you want to have one group of men in the morning and another in the afternoon, so be it. Report your progress to me at the end of each day, and let me know if you have any troubles." He gave Marcus a nod and strode away.

Behind him, Marcus barked, "Let's get this unloaded."

One relationship repaired. Lindley gazed in the direction of the schoolhouse. Now he just needed to figure out how to fix things with Bridget. That would be a lot more complicated.

On Thursday afternoon, Lindley stood over Troy's shoulder at the mine office. The boy sat at the desk, going over the summary of the ledgers he'd been working on all week.

Lindley had resisted the urge to ask. Until now. "Was Miss Greene pleased that you have started your lessons with her?" He had insisted the boy go straight from work.

"Right pleased."

He had hoped for more information about Bridget. "Did you tell her you're working in the office now?"

"Oh, yes."

Still not much of an answer. "Was she pleased about that, as well?"

He nodded. "She smiled real big."

Lindley pictured her smiling, and a smile pushed at his mouth. He missed her. He'd ruffled her sweet disposition and gentle nature, and wondered how to get them back. Hopefully, Troy working in the office would soften her toward him.

"What in tarnation's going on?"

Lindley jerked his head up and saw Mr. Keen standing in the doorway. He hadn't heard the manager enter.

Mr. Keen glanced around the room and let his gaze fall on Troy. His satchel thudded to the wooden floor. "What is the meaning of all this?"

As Lindley came around the desk, Troy scuttled out of the chair and backed into the farthest corner from the manager. Lindley stretched out his arm. "Good to have you back."

Mr. Keen shook his proffered hand. "When I said you could tidy up, I thought you'd straighten a few stacks of papers. I had no idea you'd go to such an extreme."

Lindley looked around the clean office. Everything had a place. Neat and orderly. A place someone could actually get work done in.

"And who is this?" Mr. Keen pointed to Troy. "And what was he doing in *my* chair at *my* desk?"

Lindley debated which subject to address first. The office? The *who* of Troy? Or the *why* of Troy? "Mr. Keen, this is Troy Morrison." He *was* the center of all the answers.

"Son." The manager dipped his head slightly. "Didn't I hire you to work down in the mine?"

"Yes, sir."

"Troy has been helping me in the office. He's your new assistant."

Keen jerked his gaze back to Lindley. "My what?"

"You, yourself, said that this was too much work for one man. Troy and I have been organizing things, making the place more efficient." Lindley put his hand on the back of the desk chair. "Have a seat."

Mr. Keen cautiously circled the desk and sat. "How am I supposed to find anything if you've hidden it all away?"

"Troy will get whatever you need. Just ask him for something."

The manager contemplated for a moment. "The survey report for May."

Troy scuttled to the filing cabinet and opened a drawer.

"And last year's," Keen added.

Troy pulled a file, shut the drawer and opened the one below it. He added the second file to the first and set them on the nearly clear desk. He opened each file and turned to the two May surveys.

Keen glanced from folder to folder. "Numbers are up. That's good." Then he looked up at Lindley. "Is everything this orderly?"

"Troy still has the older papers and files to organize, but he has this year's and most of last year's completed."

The boy had done well and taken to the task with vigor. He seemed to thrive on such work. The expression on his face now said he hoped to be able to continue and not go back down into the dark underground of the mine.

Lindley closed the two survey folders and set them aside so that the work Troy had been doing was visible. "We have prepared a report for you. We found multiple discrepancies. Troy, why don't you go over it for Mr. Keen?"

If the boy was going to be working directly for the manager, he needed to become comfortable talking to him. Though Troy's voice shook a little at first, he did a fine job summarizing what they had found. Lindley added only a couple of comments.

Mr. Keen's shiny scalp had turned red by the end of the presentation. "Are you telling me that every single incoming and outgoing order has an error?"

Troy widened his eyes and took a step back.

Lindley spoke up. "Not *every single* order. But most of them this year and last year. We haven't gone through everything. Troy is making an itemized list. The investors will be interested in this information."

Mr. Keen flicked his hand. "Troy, leave us."

The boy hustled out faster than a rabbit being hunted by a hawk.

Mr. Keen folded his arms. "Explain yourself."

Lindley drew in a deep breath. "Someone is stealing from the company in such small amounts that it goes unnoticed. But the accumulation of all of it adds up."

"Are you accusing me?"

"No, sir." Lindley had been glad when he could rule the manager out as the culprit. "All the discrepancies are in one person's hand. Not yours. Doesn't your foreman log a fair amount of those numbers in the ledgers?"

Mr. Keen stared hard at the report Troy had compiled. "Brady? That wretch. Stealing right from under my nose. I'll fire him today."

Lindley was glad the man could see the truth and was willing to take immediate action. "You'll be needing a new foreman."

The manager looked up at him sideways. "You applying for the position, Thompson?"

"Not me." He had a home to return to. An ache twisted in his heart. What about Bridget? He didn't want to leave without her.

"But you have someone in mind."

Lindley pulled his thoughts back to work. "Marcus Cooper. He's a good man and a natural leader to these men. He'll make an outstanding foreman."

Keen rubbed his jaw while he contemplated that. "Bring him in right away."

"I've put him in charge of a few men to repair the houses. He's doing a fine job."

Mr. Keen frowned. "What about the crew quotas?"

"I've adjusted the quotas. It won't be for long. And so far, the remaining men are almost making up the difference."

The manager nodded. "Send the boy for Cooper."

Lindley opened the door and saw Troy pacing. The poor boy. "There's nothing to worry about. Go get Mr. Cooper posthaste."

Troy ran off toward the housing.

Lindley stepped back inside the office. "About the boy. I wired the investors about hiring an assistant for you. The telegram is in the center drawer."

Keen opened it and pulled out the sheet of paper. "This pays better than breaking limestone."

"He's worth it, sir. He can enter the numbers in the ledgers, keep the office in order and run errands for you. But it'll be up to you. He'll make your job a whole lot easier."

Keen clasped his hands behind his head and leaned back in the chair. "I like the sound of that. I suppose I'll have to keep him around if I want to find anything around here."

Once Troy and Marcus had officially accepted their new positions—on a trial basis—Lindley strolled home, pleased with his accomplishments. Gabe and Dora greeted him with hugs.

His house smelled of roasting chicken, fresh bread and something sweet and cinnamony. Priscilla had grown into an exceptional cook. He knew that everything would be delicious.

But the aromas left a hollow place in the pit of his stomach. And he knew why. Bridget. She wasn't the one here cooking. Though her meals were quite tasty, Cilla was the better cook. But he didn't care. He just wanted Bridget in his kitchen.

Cilla called the children to the table, sat and waited. Everything was delicious but left a strange, empty aftertaste in his mouth. All through the meal and afterward, Cilla didn't speak to him. She spoke to the children and smiled at them, but not to him.

It was bad enough having one female angry with him, and now he had two. At least with Bridget, he kind of knew why even if he didn't understand or know how to fix it. Cilla? He hadn't a clue where to start.

He put his children to bed and came back out into the kitchen.

Cilla sat at the table, twisting a half-full glass of water around and around.

He took a deep breath. "All right. What did I do?"

She raised her lashes slowly, giving him an innocent look. "Do? You've done nothing."

He could take the easy way out and leave it at that. Instead, he pulled out a chair and sat across from her. "I can tell you're angry with me. So I must have done something to upset you." Though he couldn't think what.

"If you had done something, I wouldn't be mad at you. But you have done *nothing*. Absolutely nothing to reconcile with Bridget. You go to work and come home. It's as though you don't even care."

He raked a hand through his hair. "I don't know what to say to fix things with her."

"That is the problem with men. If you can't pick up a hammer and nail to *fix* something, you're at a loss."

A hammer and nail? He was smart enough to know that wasn't the answer, but Cilla wasn't talking about literal tools. He wished she were. He turned his hands palms up on the table. "Then help me."

"Apologize. Tell her you aren't just looking for a mother for your children."

"She doesn't think that." But what if she did? "Does she?"

"When I talked to her, she said it was about Doreen.

She wouldn't say any more than that, but what else could it be?"

Oh, it was about Doreen, all right, but not what Cilla thought. "She thinks I was wrong to enter into an arranged marriage." Had he lost her over this petty difference? He hoped not. Somehow he needed to make amends with Bridget and make her see that all arranged marriages weren't bad.

"I keep forgetting Papa orchestrated your marriage."

"As was our parents'. She only sees the bad in arrangements."

"Oh, dear." Understanding washed over Cilla's face like a wave upon the beach. "That's why she was asking if Papa would force me or any of us to marry someone we didn't want to. I thought it was just an idle conversation. But she had looked quite concerned."

"I can't change what is done. She will always see me as doing something deplorable. She will never look at me the same."

"I can't believe that. Your fight… Tell me exactly what you said and what she said." She pointed her index finger at him. "Don't leave out a word."

Lindley didn't relish verbalizing every detail. He had gone over it word for word in his head at least a dozen times a day. But to say it aloud to his baby sister was a different matter.

Cilla covered his hand with hers. "Do you love her?"

"Yes."

"Then tell me, so you can *fix* this."

He drew in a deep breath and recounted the conversation.

Cilla gaped at him in horror. "'*Maybe I will find a good husband for Dora.*' You said that? Out loud? To her?"

He had. All he could do was stare and continue to let his distress eat away at him.

Cilla propped her elbows on the table, buried her face in her hands and shook her head. She straightened. "How could you grow up in a house with four—no, five—sisters and a mother and know absolutely nothing about women?"

He had often wondered that, as well. He'd always counted himself fortunate for having escaped the turmoil of female emotions.

Doreen had explained it to him. He'd been twelve and uninterested in girls when Rachel, his oldest sister, had married. He hadn't been interested in the nuances of the female heart. Then he had been suddenly betrothed, so feminine emotions had become irrelevant. Something he no longer needed to work at learning. Doreen had understood him better than he understood himself.

Alice, one year younger than him, would tell him he was a stupid boy who wasn't worth explaining anything to. He was always tempted to argue the *stupid* bit with her, but then he risked her explaining things he had no interest in.

He wished he had.

Now he needed to work at figuring out the female heart. "So if I apologize for saying I'll choose Dora's husband, that will fix things with Bridget?" Hadn't he tried that, and it hadn't worked? "I thought she was upset because I entered into an arranged marriage."

"Neither, dear brother. It's about her feelings."

"She's angry at me. That's how she's feeling." That much he'd figured out.

Cilla shook her head and glanced heavenward. "That's not what I mean. Just because your marriage was good and Mama and Papa's is good doesn't mean they all are."

"I know that."

"But that's not what you were telling her. You were telling her that women's feelings don't matter and men know best."

"I never said that!"

"Read between the lines, dear brother. Women have few options but to do what men tell them. So you were telling her women are unimportant. Therefore, *she* is unimportant."

"Really?" The workings of the female mind were boggling. "I don't think that at all. She's very important."

She leaned toward him over the table. "Then you must make sure she knows that."

"So what am I to do? Apologize for not considering her feelings? Tell her she's important?"

She nodded. "Grovel. And it wouldn't hurt to get her a small gift. A bottle of perfume or something that makes her feel feminine."

Lindley remembered something at the general store that he had wanted to purchase for Bridget, but couldn't when people thought he was a simple miner. Everyone would have known he couldn't afford anything beyond basic provisions and would have wondered who he really was. He hadn't been able to take the risk then, but now he could make the purchase. "So what *exactly* should I say?"

"I can't tell you what to say. The words would never come out right, and Bridget would know they weren't real. She would feel it." Cilla reached across the table and touched his chest. "Speak from your heart. If she says something that doesn't make sense to you, tell her you don't understand but you're trying to. You want to." She stood and walked toward the hall but stopped and turned. "And don't forget to kiss her." She gave an impish smile and headed off to the bedroom she was sharing with Dora.

Kiss her? Gladly!

But first he had to beg her forgiveness.

He'd been praying all week for a solution to his dilemma

with Bridget. Never would he have guessed that his baby sister would hold the answers. The Lord did work in mysterious ways.

Chapter 14

The week sailed by, and Friday came, the last day of the school year. A sadness settled on Bridget to be turning her students out into the world. Of course, she would see them around town, and most of them would be back in the fall.

"Before I let you all go, I just want to say that I have enjoyed teaching you. Have a pleasant summer."

The students rose in excited chatter and a clatter of boots scuffing on the worn wooden floor. Only Dora and Gabe remained seated. They would wait inside for their aunt.

When the other children had all left, Cilla entered but stayed at the back of the room. "Dora, Gabe, time to go."

Dora ran to her aunt, who scooped her up in her arms. "Come on, Gabe."

Gabe had his head down, rolling his forehead back and forth on the desk.

Cilla moved up beside him and wiggled her hand. "Come on."

Gabe stared at her a moment, scooted out from his desk and ran, but not to the back of the room. He headed straight for Bridget and threw his arms around her waist. He didn't say a word.

Bridget patted his back. "What's wrong?"

He shook his head, rubbing his face against her waist.

She loosened his grip and knelt. "Gabe?"

The boy hooked his arms around her neck and held her tight. "I don't want school to be over."

She hugged him back and then pulled him away so she could look him in the eyes. "It'll be all right. You'll have a nice summer and be back in school in the fall." But not likely her classroom. He would go back to his home on some other part of the island. She grabbed a volume about animals from the corner of her desk. "Would you like to take this with you and look at it over the summer?" She knew he wouldn't be able to read most of the text, but he would try. And he and Dora could enjoy the drawings.

Gabe nodded and hugged the book to his chest.

Cilla wiggled her free hand at Gabe. "Come along now."

Bridget used the corner of her desk to pull herself up. "You aren't going to stay awhile?"

Lindley's sister had visited with her every afternoon this week. But wasn't going to today?

"Not today."

Bridget's heart contracted. She liked the young woman.

Cilla tilted her head to the back of the room. "You have another visitor." She gave Bridget a brief hug and left with the children.

Bridget's heart nearly stopped at the sight of Lindley standing at the back of the room. She had worn a plain white shirtwaist and hunter green skirt. If she had known Lindley would be calling, she would have worn something nicer. She had prayed for an opportunity to speak with him.

He strode up the aisle, working the brim of his hat. He looked nervous, as if he didn't know what to say.

She hoped he hadn't come to tell her goodbye. "I'm sorry for getting so upset about the whole arranged-marriage business. I misspoke. It wasn't my place."

He blinked several times before he found his voice.

"You really shouldn't make an apology this easy for a gentleman. Don't you know you're supposed to make the man grovel? Now I'm at a loss for words."

That meant he hadn't come to say farewell. She breathed easier. "Is that what you came to do? Grovel?"

"If need be."

Her heart danced. "By all means, don't let me stop you."

"I came to beg for your forgiveness for getting defensive. Some arranged marriages can be horrendous. I was one of the fortunate ones. I didn't consider your feelings. And you *are* important to me. I never meant to suggest otherwise."

"I accept your gracious apology and happily grant you forgiveness."

He fumbled in his coat pocket. "I brought you a peace offering." He held out a gift wrapped in an embroidered handkerchief, tied with a pink ribbon. "The wrapping is part of the gift, too."

She accepted the present, pulled the ribbon free and folded back the corners of the cloth. A tortoiseshell hair comb with sterling-silver adornment. "It's beautiful." She turned it over in her hands.

"Why don't you put it in your hair?"

She raised her gaze to him. "Would you?" Her skin prickled at the intimacy of the request.

He took the comb and poked it several times at her hair but never well enough for it to stay.

So she covered his hand with hers and helped him work the comb in on the side of her head. When it was in place, she let her fingers slide across the back of his hand as she lowered hers. "Does it look all right?"

He drew in a quick breath. "Beautiful." He shifted his gaze to her eyes and then her mouth. "Very beautiful."

Her breathing came in irregular puffs as he leaned closer.

Finally, he pressed his lips to hers.

She looped her arms around him, and he held her, as well. She felt safe in his embrace. She couldn't think of any other place she would rather be.

He pulled away. "Cilla told me I had to do that."

"Cilla? And no other reason?"

His mouth pulled up on one side. "Oh, I had my own reasons."

"I should hope so."

"And just so you know, I have no plans to choose Dora's future husband. The thought of Dora marrying someday is hard to imagine. So I may not let her marry at all."

"When she bats those big brown eyes of hers and tells you she's in love—"

"I'll lock her in her room."

She bit her lip between her teeth to tame her smile. "When was the last time you denied your daughter anything? You are like bread dough in her hands."

He took Bridget's hand. "I recall putting her off when she demanded I love you and marry you."

Love and marriage? She hadn't imagined he'd considered such things. She had thought of them often. Her cheeks heated. "Putting off is not the same as denied." She hoped he didn't let the important subject drop.

"No, it's not."

He had put Dora's demands off before. Was he still?

Lindley wanted to stand there and take in every feature of Bridget's face. From her green eyes and long eyelashes to her rosy lips and fair skin. Was it too soon to tell her he loved her?

Bridget glanced away.

He'd made her nervous.

She met his gaze once more. "I truly am sorry for my

reaction. I had no right. It really is none of my business how you raise your children."

He gazed at her intently for a moment longer. He spoke in a husky voice. "I'm hoping it will be."

"Will be?" Her eyes brightened, and her breath seemed to catch.

He sensed she understood his meaning. And she appeared to be happy about it. Was this the right time and place? The schoolhouse? "Bridget...I—"

"Gabe. Dora. No."

Lindley turned to see his children racing up the aisle.

Cilla hurried behind them. "I'm sorry. They got away from me."

Gabe stopped at Bridget's hip and leaned against her. His son missed his mother. Bridget would make a very good mother for his children. But that was not why he was interested in her. He *loved* her. And he hadn't gotten to tell her. "You'll still go with me to the party tomorrow, won't you?"

And there it was again. That reluctance in her expression when he'd asked her the first time. She was happy one moment and then she wasn't. Did she not believe his apology? Or was her look one of apprehension, having never been to such a formal event?

Cilla spoke up. "Of course she'll go. Right, Bridget?"

A wan smile pulled at Bridget's mouth. "I would be honored to attend with you."

The next day, Bridget sat in a kitchen chair in front of the oval mirror attached to her bureau. Cilla stood behind her, arranging Bridget's hair. The girl had arrived in the middle of the afternoon to help Bridget ready herself for the party with Lindley and the investors. She was like a lady's maid.

Bridget had convinced herself she wouldn't know anyone in attendance, except Lindley. She would focus on having the most wonderful time. She hadn't been to a party like this in years.

Cilla pinned up another curl and tucked in the comb from Lindley. "All done. Do you like it?"

Bridget twisted her head from side to side. "It's lovely. I couldn't have done this by myself." She had wanted to plait her hair in a more elaborate style like this but had resigned herself to her usual chignon with a few extra curls around her face. "Will you help me into my dress?"

"Of course." Cilla held the pink silk dress low to the floor.

Bridget stepped into the opening. Cilla tucked in the bottom of the petticoat and pulled the dress up so Bridget could put her arms through the sleeves. Cilla deftly buttoned up the back. So much easier than when Bridget had done so herself a week ago. It had taken her an hour and the use of her shoe buttonhook.

In a swish of fabric, Bridget faced Cilla. "Do I look all right?"

"Like a dream."

"You don't think Lindley will mind my wearing the same dress I wore to supper last week, do you?"

"You will render him speechless with your beauty. But I have an idea." Cilla opened the wardrobe. "My, you have a lot of clothes."

"They are all years old. But the cloth is still in good condition. It would be a shame to waste them."

Cilla thumbed through the dresses, skirts and shirtwaists. She came out with a black velvet sash with a matching rosette and a long black lace shawl. "Do you have black gloves?"

"Top drawer."

Cilla retrieved those, as well. "Put these on."

Bridget did while Cilla tied the sash around her waist and then pinned the rosette at her neckline. She draped the black shawl around Bridget's back with one end over each elbow. She turned back to the bureau, retrieved a black velvet choker with a pink cameo and fastened that around Bridget's throat. Then she stepped back and sighed. "He won't even notice that it's the same gown."

Bridget turned to the mirror. The black accents against the pink were stunning. The fingerless black lace gloves came up to her elbows, where the sleeves ended, giving the illusion that the dress had black lace sleeves. Bridget never would have thought to accent the dress with black. The girl was a genius. "But surely he'll know it's the same."

Cilla shook her head. "This is my brother we're talking about. Trust me, he won't have the slightest notion. I've got to run along. Have a good time tonight."

"You're not staying until Lindley arrives?"

"Can't. If I don't leave, my brother won't be able to come. I have to look after the little ones." Cilla gave her a gentle hug and dashed out the door.

Bridget looked again into the mirror. Certainly Lindley would see that it was the same dress. But she didn't care. She felt like Cinderella in *The Little Glass Slipper* going to a fancy ball.

Chapter 15

Before long, Lindley knocked.

Bridget took a deep breath and opened the door.

He cut a dashing figure in his fine evening suit. "You… you look…beautiful. No. More than beautiful."

Her breath caught at his earnest compliment. "Thank you."

Cilla had been wonderful to fuss her hair into this fancy arrangement and decorate it with the comb he'd given her. She had been told this type of style complemented her features. And he noticed. But did he realize the dress was the same? Or had Cilla successfully camouflaged it?

"You look dapper yourself."

He tugged at the lapels of his coat. "It is nice, but I prefer comfortable everyday clothes." He swept his arm to motion behind him. "I brought a carriage."

"You really didn't have to."

"I want you to arrive in style. Besides, it could rain before the evening is over." He escorted her to the carriage, helped her up and climbed in himself. He snapped the reins, and the horse lurched the rig forward.

"Did you rent this?"

He shook his head. "It belongs to my father-in-law."

Her breath caught. "Is he going to be in attendance tonight?"

"Of course. He's one of the investors. Don't worry. He'll like you."

"I'm not so sure about that."

"Why wouldn't he?"

"Because of his daughter."

"Doreen is gone."

"Yes, and he might not like the idea of you and another woman. He may see me as replacing her."

Lindley was silent a moment, no doubt contemplating her comment. "I'm sure it'll be all right." But his tone wasn't so confident. "I'll talk to him. It'll be fine."

Was he trying to convince her or himself? Bridget's insides twisted. *Lord, please don't let him think I'm trying to replace his daughter.*

Lindley pulled up to the front of the hotel, handed off the carriage to a stable boy and helped Bridget down. "Don't worry about a thing."

She would try. Then an unbidden thought kicked up her apprehension. What if she had met his father-in-law? She hadn't thought to ask his name. *Mercy.* Could she claim an illness and return home? This party meant a lot to Lindley. She didn't want to spoil it for him either by going or not.

After tonight, she would find a good time to tell him. She didn't want to ruin his evening.

Music and voices floated out the entrance into the cool evening air. Lindley ushered her inside, took her shawl and handed it over to the cloakroom clerk. He escorted her into the main ballroom.

She forced a deep, calming breath into her lungs. *Lord, make this evening go well.*

Lindley surveyed the room. "There he is."

She knew he meant his late wife's father. Was she ready for this?

He guided her across the room to a portly man with

stark white hair, a mustache and a severe expression. "Miss Bridget Greene, this is my father-in-law, Gabriel Andrews."

She'd never met this man. She let out a relieved breath as she bobbed a quick curtsy. "Pleased to meet you, Mr. Andrews." So, Gabe had been named after his grandfather.

He regarded her and spoke in a level voice. "So you are the Miss Greene my grandchildren speak so fondly of."

She couldn't tell from his tone if that was good or bad. "They are sweet children."

Mr. Andrews narrowed his eyes, scrutinizing her.

Lindley cleared his throat. "Miss Greene is their teacher."

Mr. Andrews swung a silencing glance to Lindley and then looked back to her. "May I have this dance?" He held out his hand.

Bridget didn't know how she could refuse, so she put her hand in his. As she was being led away, she looked back at Lindley, who gave her an encouraging nod. But she could see the worry in his face.

Mr. Andrews was proficient at waltzing. But the way he studied her face unnerved her. This was the man who'd negotiated a husband for his daughter. She kept a genial smile in place as though his inspection didn't bother her. Certainly he had questions. Was he going to ask them?

"So, my granddaughter talked her way into your class-room."

That was not the first thing she'd expected him to say. "Yes. She arrived during recess. I couldn't send her off on her own. She behaved herself well enough."

"Yes, when she wants something, she can be as sweet as sugared molasses."

"Isn't molasses sweet enough without sugaring it?"

"My Dora is even sweeter."

Ah, his Dora. He obviously loved his grandchildren very much.

"Doreen was my only child. So Gabe and Dora are my only grandchildren. They deserve…"

"Mr. Andrews, I'm not trying to replace your daughter."

His expression softened. "That's not what I was getting at. My Francesca passed away soon after we lost Doreen. My grandchildren deserve a lady's touch in their lives. Oh, they have Lindley's sisters and mother, but it is not the same as having a woman in their home, caring for them day after day."

She didn't know what to say to that. Was he giving her and Lindley his blessing? Not that Lindley had proposed.

"Don't get me wrong. Lindley does a fine job with them. But a mother's love is different. Gentler, softer, nurturing. Wouldn't you agree?"

She couldn't really say. Her own mother hadn't the time for her. Although not all that nurturing, Mother had been gentler and softer, Bridget supposed. But she had seen it with the mothers of her students. "I suppose they are."

He deftly guided her around another couple. "I nearly lost Doreen when she was ten. Lindley saved her from being run down by a charging freight wagon. Poor boy was injured."

"Lindley told me. Then you and his father arranged their marriage." Oh, dear. She shouldn't have said that. She just didn't understand what kind of father could do that. And Mr. Andrews seemed to adore his daughter.

"Oh, I was against it at first. With Doreen being deaf, I was going to keep her under my wing for the rest of her life to protect her. My wife convinced me that would not be good for any of us. So Warren and I came to an agreement with the stipulation that when they grew up, if either of them were in love with someone else or they really didn't like each other, they didn't have to marry. Though we didn't tell them that."

So he wasn't coldhearted. He was actually looking out for his daughter's well-being.

"Lindley treated Doreen well. He took good care of her. And she loved him so very much. If I'd had my way, she never would have gotten married and had the pleasure of having children she loved as much as any mother could. And she was good for him. He was a bit awkward and shy with girls. Don't know why, growing up in a house full of them. Or maybe that's why."

The waltz ended, but Mr. Andrews didn't release her or walk her off the dance floor. Instead, he said, "Another."

That went against good etiquette.

"Please." He flashed Dora's smile.

She relaxed. "I'd love to."

The next waltz started up, and he led her around the floor. "Tell me about yourself."

"Not much to tell. I teach at the school."

"Have you always lived on the islands?"

Her stomach tightened. She didn't like this line of questions. "No."

"Where's your family from?"

"My grandparents lived in Illinois." Truth but not all of it.

"I visited Illinois once. I rather liked it there."

Bridget managed to keep the conversation away from her background except where it pertained to the children and school.

At the end of the tune, Mr. Andrews escorted her off the floor. He bowed over her hand. "Thank you for the delightful waltz."

"The pleasure was mine, Mr. Andrews." She accepted the offered cup of punch from Lindley and sipped.

"Please call me Gabriel."

"Certainly. And you may call me Bridget."

Gabriel turned to Lindley. "You have a lovely lady here."

"Thank you, sir."

Gabriel motioned with his hand. "Come with me. There is someone I want you to meet." He led the way.

Bridget was going to remain put, but Lindley took her arm and guided her around the room with him. Lindley kept his voice low. "So, you won over my father-in-law."

"I really didn't do much. He seems like a sweet man."

"I knew he would be taken with you."

Gabriel stopped near a tall, black-haired man who was talking with another man.

Bridget sipped her punch. She had been so focused on getting ready for tonight, she had forgotten to drink much water today.

The men finished their conversation, and the tall man shifted his attention to Gabriel and thrust out his hand. "Gabriel, good to see you."

"Zachariah, I'd like you to meet Lindley Thompson. He's my right-hand man. He's the one who's been working here at the mine for the past few months. And this is his sweetheart, Bridget Greene. And this is Zachariah March."

Bridget choked on her punch. March? Oh, dear. She coughed.

Lindley patted her back. "Are you all right?"

She nodded. "Fine." She cleared her throat. "Just swallowed wrong." Where could she run to and hide? But it was already too late.

Mr. March took her hand and bowed over it. "Miss… *Greene*, was it?"

He knew it wasn't, but he hadn't given her away. Yet. "Mr. March." She struggled to give a polite smile.

"It is a delight and pleasure to meet you. Please call me Zach." He winked.

She gave a nod of assent. "And you may call me Bridget. If you gentlemen will excuse me, please." She walked away, her stomach twisting violently. Though Zach's wife was her friend, she didn't know him well enough to know if he would keep her secret.

The room seemed to grow suddenly hot and stifling, so she hurried outside for some fresh air.

A groomsman met her gaze. "May I help you, miss?"

"No, I'm fine." She slowed her pace and strolled to the end of the wide porch. She drew in several deep breaths to calm herself.

What if Zach was telling Lindley and Gabriel she wasn't really Miss Greene? Maybe she shouldn't have left the men alone. Should she go back inside? Or just leave?

Coming had been a bad idea. She should have confessed to Lindley. She had tried to at the schoolhouse yesterday but had been interrupted. If she had told him, then she would know if his feelings were true. Now, if he found out from someone else, from Zach, he would only feel betrayed.

She had to get away from here. She would pack her things and leave before Zach could tell anyone about her.

No. She had to find Lindley and tell him before anyone else did. He deserved to hear the truth from her.

No. Not at the party. That would spoil his evening. Unless her past didn't bother him. But not telling him would bother him. She had to at least try to talk to Lindley.

"Bridget!"

She stopped at the sound of Zach's voice and turned slowly to him. She was caught.

He strolled up to her. "Bridget *Greene*." He tested her name in his mouth. "It has a nice ring to it. But then, so does Bridget *Thompson*."

He was toying with her.

"Are you in love with him?"

What did that matter? "What do you want?"

"You didn't answer my question."

Dare she answer? "Yes, I love him."

"Does he love you?"

What did he intend to do with the information? "Yes."

A broad smile broke across his face. "Good. I'll tell Fina. You really should write her more."

She hadn't dared for fear a letter might get intercepted by someone who would divulge her whereabouts.

"Don't look so worried. I won't tell anyone."

"You won't? Why not?"

"Fina would be impossible to live with. When she's angry, she has a *very* long memory. It's best to let her have her way. As stubborn as a mule."

She relaxed at his friendly tone. "I just might tell her you said that."

"It's nothing she doesn't already know."

"Didn't she come with you?" She would love to see her dear friend.

"Regrettably, no. She came down with a terrible stomach ailment the day before we were to leave. Doctor ordered bed rest."

"Nothing too serious, I hope?"

"She was already feeling better, but the trip would have worn her out."

"Give her my best. And tell her I'll write soon."

"I will. She will be sorry she couldn't come." He offered her his arm. "Now let me escort you back inside. Unless there is someone else you were running away from."

Not that she knew of. She took his arm.

Lindley's turn to dance with Bridget. He bowed in front of her. "May I have this dance?"

She gave him a playful smile. "I thought you didn't dance."

Lindley smiled and guided her to the middle of the floor. "I'll make an exception for you."

She put her left hand on his shoulder and raised her other one for him to take.

He liked having her in his arms. His pulse picked up speed. Leading her in the first steps of the waltz, he wondered where she had learned the dance. When would a simple schoolteacher have had the opportunity?

After once around the floor, he asked, "Zachariah March. You know him?"

She took a quick breath. "'Twas your father-in-law who introduced him."

He hadn't missed her slight hesitation before she'd answered. And she hadn't exactly answered him. He wouldn't have thought much about the introduction had he not seen the two talking moments later on the porch. Then he had thought back to Zach's comment. *Miss* Greene, *was it?*

The two knew each other. But how?

Chapter 16

Lindley walked to the schoolhouse on Monday to see Bridget. She had said she would be cleaning the building today.

On Friday, when he'd apologized, he hadn't spoken from his heart as Cilla had told him to do. He had merely said words. And he hadn't groveled nearly enough. Hardly at all. Bridget had made apologizing easy. And he hadn't told her how he felt about her.

Now Zachariah March had shown up. He had spoken to her in a rather friendly manner after church. And he meant something to her. Lindley just didn't know how. But if he didn't want to lose her to this man, he needed to let Bridget know exactly how he felt and what his intentions were.

She came out the door with a bucket and tossed the water onto the ground next to the stoop. She had a scarf tied around her auburn hair and wore a plain gray shirt and brown plaid skirt. Not a very attractive outfit. She had obviously dressed for her day of cleaning. She wiped the back of her hand across her forehead.

He sighed. She was so beautiful no matter what she wore. He moved toward her.

She looked up, grimaced and took a step back as though to flee inside. She smoothed a hand down her skirt, swiped off her head scarf and touched her hair.

He stopped at the foot of the steps. "You look beautiful."

"No, I don't."

"Yes, you do."

"The Good Book says, 'Thou shalt not lie.'"

He clapped his hand over his heart. "'Tis no lie. You are beautiful to me."

"I'm a mess."

He took the pail from her, set it on the top step and grasped her hand. He wanted to ask her again about Zachariah March but suspected that conversation wouldn't end any better than the one about his arranged marriage. "When I came to apologize on Friday, I didn't say all I wanted to."

Cilla had told him to speak from his heart. He hadn't really understood then what she meant, but he did now.

He pointed to the steps. "Would you like to sit?"

"What I'd like to do is run and hide." She glanced at her head scarf she had gripped tightly in her free hand. "Very well." She sat.

He removed his hat and sat next to her, keeping her hand firmly in his. "You needn't worry. No amount of dirt can hide how pretty you are. As you told me the first time I came to your house to retrieve my children, 'It's just dirt.'"

She dropped her scarf on her lap. "You're right. I'm being foolish."

"I like that it matters to you how you look in my presence."

Her cheeks turned pink. "Now I really feel foolish."

He caressed the back of her hand with his thumb. "Please don't."

Did he have the courage to tell her? He wanted to. He took a deep breath. From his heart. "I love you."

She smiled and then frowned. "Oh, Lindley. I...I need to tell—"

"Shh." He knew she might not feel the same way about him yet. He didn't want to rush her. He cupped her face in his hands. "You don't have to say anything." He pressed his lips to hers.

She didn't resist and kissed him back. She wouldn't have responded like that if Zachariah March meant something to her romantically, would she?

He pulled back. "I love you so much. It's okay if you don't know yet. I don't want to pressure you. I just wanted— no, *needed* you to know how I felt." Now did he also have the courage to ask? He hoped this was the right time. "I never contemplated marrying again after Doreen died. But you have made me consider things I had never thought of before."

Her expression held both hope and concern. Joy and pain.

"You don't have to answer right away, but I want you to know how much you mean to me. I want you to be my wife. Will you—"

A high-pitched, bloodcurdling scream from somewhere in town split the air.

A chill coiled around Lindley's spine. He jerked his head around. "Dora!"

"No. How do you know?"

"I just do." He took off at a run. Fear stampeded through him in a rush, pushing him faster. The impact of each footfall vibrated up his body, stabbing him in the heart.

"Mr. Thompson!" Troy ran down the street toward him. The boy stopped in front of him and put his hands on his thighs, doubling over to catch his breath.

Lindley put a hand on the boy's shoulder. "Take it easy. Catch your breath. Then tell me what's wrong." He prayed it wasn't Dora. But why else would the boy be coming to him? Not Gabe. *Lord, please let my children be safe.*

Troy sucked in several ragged breaths. "You have to come— Quick— Your daughter— Dora— A horse— She's hurt— Hurt bad."

Lindley's heart and chest twisted into a tight, painful knot. He had hoped he was wrong. Not his little girl. "Where?"

Troy sucked in another breath. "Hotel."

Lindley ran as fast as he could, pain shooting through his bad leg. But he would not stop. Would not slow until he knew Dora was safe. But Troy had already told him she wasn't.

In front of the hotel, a crowd huddled in the street.

He couldn't hear Dora crying. Certainly, if she were hurt, she would be crying. Maybe she was fine, and Troy had overreacted. He pushed his way through the mass.

The doctor and Cilla knelt beside the motionless form of his daughter.

Lindley's throat constricted, nearly cutting off his air. She wasn't moving. His baby wasn't moving. He fell to his knees. No! Not his little girl. He smoothed blond hair from her pinched face.

"I'm sorry, Lindley," Cilla cried. "I only looked away for a moment."

He couldn't look at his sister right now. His gaze fixed on Dora's labored breathing. Up-down. Up-down. Up-down.

The doctor put his hand on Lindley's shoulder. "I think she fainted from the pain."

"Pain?" he choked out.

Dr. Unger pointed to Dora's leg.

Lindley gasped at her willowy, stockinged calf bent in the wrong place. His own leg shot with pain. He knew the kind of agony she was in. His boyhood memory of writhing in the street crashed over him, knocking the wind out of his lungs. He struggled to breathe. "What happened?"

"Horse spooked. Reared," a voice in the crowd said.

Another voice said, "Fortunate it was her leg and not her head."

Lindley glared at the man. "Fortunate?" There was nothing fortunate about a broken leg. His own leg throbbed with stabbing pain. Was it real? Or just the memory?

"I'm sorry," Cilla said. "I'm sorry. I'm so, so sorry."

Dr. Unger cleared his throat. "Let's get her to my office."

Two men brought a wide plank. "We can carry her on this." The crowd parted, and they set the board next to Dora's still form.

The doctor and another man reached for Dora.

Lindley pushed their hands away. "Don't touch her!"

Out of breath, Bridget finally reached a crowd in front of the hotel. Gabe stood a few feet back, silent tears running down his face. Bridget knelt beside him and touched his arm. "Are you all right, Gabe?"

He jerked away and ran off.

"Gabe!" She wanted to go to Lindley, who she presumed was in the middle of the throng, but someone needed to see to Gabe.

Troy came up beside her. "I'll go after him."

"Thank you," Bridget said.

"I'll make sure he's all right. Safe." Troy trotted off in the direction Gabe had gone.

Bridget pushed her way through the crowd until she could see Dora lying on the dirt. She slapped her hand over her mouth.

Kneeling beside his daughter, Lindley held her little hand in one of his large ones and stroked her hair with the other.

Oh, dear! She wasn't— Bridget didn't want to think such a thing. So she stared at the girl's chest. It rose and fell in short, difficult breaths. She was alive. But what had happened?

Cilla sat in the dirt across from Bridget, tears streaming down her face. "I'm sorry." She shifted her gaze to Dora's leg.

Bridget looked as well and gasped. The leg was severely broken. The poor child must be in so much pain. No wonder her breathing came in catches. Tears sprang to Bridget's eyes.

"I'm so, so sorry." Cilla rocked back and forth.

The doctor, on the other side of Dora, reached for her little arm. "Mr. Thomp—"

"I said don't touch her!"

The doctor withdrew his hand and glanced up at Bridget. "We need to get her to my office."

Bridget blinked away her tears. This was no time for her to cry. Lindley needed her. She crouched beside him and gently placed her hand on his arm. "We need to get her out of the street. Let them move her."

He was silent for a moment and then nodded. "I'll do it." He tucked one hand under her neck. The other hesitated by her knees.

Bridget supported the injured leg at the ankle and knee. She couldn't see any blood. That was good. That meant the bone hadn't broken through the skin.

Lindley lifted his daughter tentatively and gingerly laid her on the plank.

Even though unconscious, Dora moaned.

"I'm so, so, so sorry," Cilla said again and again.

Bridget shushed her while making sure to keep the injured leg as still as possible. Any movement could cause further damage to the little girl. Irreparable damage.

Two men picked up the board, one at each end.

Lindley stayed beside his daughter's head, staring at her face as though he couldn't bear to view her injury.

Bridget continued to support the bent calf.

The procession took its time moving across the uneven ground to keep Dora stable. Part of the crowd followed, whispering in hushed tones.

Dr. Unger opened his office door. The crowd fell away except for Cilla. Lindley and Bridget had to let go of Dora so the board would fit through the doorway.

The doctor directed the men through another doorway. "Set the whole lot on the exam table. I don't want to move her unnecessarily yet. That could cause more damage."

The men lowered the board to the table and left.

Dr. Unger pointed. "The three of you should wait in the other room."

"I'm staying with my daughter." Lindley's tone left no room for argument. He turned to Bridget and his sister. "You two can stay, as well."

Dr. Unger heaved a sigh to show his displeasure. "As long as neither of you gets in my way or faints. I don't need two more patients." He rolled up his sleeves.

Lindley turned to Bridget and his sister again. "Will you two be all right?"

"Yes." Bridget didn't want Lindley to be alone. She wanted to support him. He must be so torn up inside.

Cilla's face was the color of the sheet covering the exam table.

Bridget put a hand on her arm. "Can you go see to Gabe? Troy Morrison went after him."

The girl nodded, seemingly relieved to have something to do away from the doctor's office. She rushed out.

After the doctor washed his hands and toweled them

dry, he directed Bridget to carefully remove Dora's shoe and stocking.

Why hadn't he asked Lindley to do it? But when Bridget looked at the anguish on his face, she understood. She took a deep breath to steady herself as she performed the task. She looked away from the bruised leg, which was already swelling.

"It's fortunate the bone didn't break the skin. I won't sugarcoat it. The break is bad. She could lose the lower part of her leg."

"No!" Lindley shook his head. "No, no, no…"

Bridget stared at Dora's thin leg. It couldn't be that bad. "Surely you can save it."

The doctor shrugged as he dabbed chloroform on a cloth.

Bridget recognized the smell. "What are you going to do?"

"For now, I'll straighten her leg and splint it." He put the cloth to Dora's mouth. "Can you make sure she doesn't wake?" He handed the bottle to her. "Just a drop on the cloth every so often. Watch her breathing. She's small, so she doesn't need much."

Bridget stood by Dora's head and kept the cloth in place. She glanced up at Lindley.

He held his daughter's small hand in both of his. His ashen complexion held the depth of his concern. He kept his eyes fixed on Dora's face as though that would make everything all right.

Poor man.

Bridget shifted her focus to the child's breathing. Steady. Then to Dr. Unger.

With a delicate touch, he probed the break. He looked up at her and shook his head.

The leg can't be saved?

She shook her head, as well. He'd better not dare suggest amputation.

"The bone is shattered into too many pieces. It will never mend."

Lindley didn't move or seem to register what the doctor implied.

Bridget covered Lindley's hand with hers and spoke in a soft, calm voice. "He wants to take her leg." Out of the corner of her vision, she saw the doctor nod.

Lindley looked up at her, dazed. "What? Take it where?" He seemed to begin to focus.

"He wants to cut it—"

Lindley jerked his gaze to Dr. Unger. "No! No, you won't!"

Bridget was pleased with Lindley's decision. It hadn't been her place to say one way or the other. Though she would have fought for Dora's leg if Lindley could not.

"It's too broken to repair itself. It will just turn gangrenous."

Lindley shook his head and swung his gaze to her, pleading in his eyes. He wanted her to make everything all right even though he had no idea it was actually within her power to do so.

Conflicted about what to do, knowing either decision would have its own set of consequences, she made her decision and spoke. "Dr. Unger might not have the expertise for this kind of complicated procedure, but I know a doctor who does."

"You do?" Hope sprang to Lindley's brown eyes like a lone flickering candle in the darkness. "Will he do it?"

Bridget was sure she could convince him. She nodded.

"How far is it? Can Dora make the trip?"

Dr. Unger shook his head. "I don't recommend moving

her in her present state. She's already in shock. It could cause more damage to her leg."

Lindley glared at the man. "You will not stop me from helping my daughter."

"Dr. Unger is right. I can telegram the doctor, asking him to come."

"Will he come all the way here?"

"Yes." *She* could get him to come.

Dr. Unger shook his head. "And what do you propose doing with the child in the meantime?"

Lindley looked from the doctor to Bridget, panic etched in his features.

Bridget could tell that he wasn't able to think clearly in his distress. "The *child's* name is Dora. Splint the leg as you were going to and give her something for the pain."

The doctor frowned and looked as though he might refuse. "I suppose." He stepped away from Dora to get supplies.

Lindley gave Bridget a look of gratitude.

She touched Lindley's arm. "I'm going to send the telegram. Don't let Dr. Unger do anything more than put on a splint."

Lindley nodded. "I won't let her lose her leg. I won't!"

She prayed he held to that conviction, and the doctor didn't try to persuade him otherwise in her absence. In Lindley's distress, he might be easily swayed if the doctor insisted Dora's life might be in danger. Or that Lindley wouldn't realize what the doctor was doing until it was too late.

She stepped into the other room. Cilla, Gabe and Troy sat on a bench like a trio waiting for the gallows. She was glad Troy had found Gabe and brought him back so quickly.

Cilla stood. "How is she?"

Bridget looked from Lindley's sister to Gabe and drew the girl across the room. "Her leg is badly broken. She needs a doctor who is experienced with this kind of injury. Can you go in with your brother while I send a telegram?"

Concern etched the girl's face, her complexion pallid. "I—I...I don't know."

Lindley needed someone with him for support. He was too distraught and vulnerable to be on his own to cope with his erratic emotions and Dr. Unger.

"This doctor wants to cut off Dora's leg and be done with it."

"What?" Cilla squared her shoulders. "He better not try. I'll make sure he doesn't." She marched into the room where Lindley and Dora were.

Good girl.

A lot of people didn't think they could do things until faced with them, especially when a loved one's life was at stake.

Bridget turned to Gabe and Troy.

Gabe looked wounded himself. "I'm sorry. I didn't mean for Dora to get hurt."

"It's not your fault."

"We didn't mean to scare the horse. Is Dora going to be all right? Is she going to die?"

"No. She will be fine." If the doctor would come. She turned to Troy. "Thank you for finding him. Can you stay here with him for a little while?"

"Of course."

"Thank you. I'll be back as soon as I can." She rushed out. The sooner she got the telegram sent, the sooner the doctor would arrive, the better for Dora.

She hurried to the telegraph office. "I need to send a telegram."

The operator slid her a tablet of paper. "Write your message and who it is to and where you want it sent. Keep it short and as concise as possible."

She wrote her message. "Mark it urgent. I'll pay extra to have it delivered immediately. And I'll wait here for a reply."

He took the pad. "As you wish." He sat at his desk and tapped out her message on his machine.

Click. Click. Clickety-click.

That would put an end to Lindley's almost proposal. Her answer set before she'd ever met him.

Lindley wanted to crumple to the floor. His little sister's presence bolstered him. *Lord, heal Dora. Make her better.*

Cilla stood sentry over Dora's injured leg, peppering the doctor with questions about his every move.

He'd never realized his baby sister possessed such strength. She had always been a bit pampered, with everyone else doing for her. He still thought of her as the tantrum-throwing eight-year-old she was when he left home. But she had grown into a strong and beautiful young lady.

Dora's leg was splinted between narrow boards and wrapped with strips of cloth to keep it all in place. The doctor had given her morphine, telling Lindley it would make her sleep.

Lindley wished Bridget was back. She gave him strength.

Chapter 17

Lindley sat at Dora's side all night. His daughter rarely woke, and when she did, she was in pain, so she was given another dose of morphine. Bridget stayed with them, curled up on the bench in the other room. Cilla had taken Gabe home.

The following morning, Bridget left early and returned an hour later with a distinguished man who appeared to be in his late forties or early fifties. His sandy-brown hair was peppered with gray. His erect stance gave him command of any room, including this one.

Bridget made the introductions. "Dr. Grayson, this is Dr. Unger. And this is Lindley Thompson and his daughter, Dora."

Lindley stretched out his hand. "Dr. Gra—"

The doctor waved him off and zeroed in on Dora's leg, stepping over to the exam table. "How long ago was the accident?" He looked but didn't touch.

"Less than twenty-four hours," Bridget said.

Without glancing up, he held out his hand toward the other doctor. "Scissors."

Dr. Unger looked taken aback at being treated like a mere nurse, but he slapped a pair of surgical scissors into Dr. Grayson's hand.

The doctor snipped through the bandages holding the

splint in place one layer at a time, careful not to touch the leg with the scissors. With gentle fingertips, he pulled back the cloth strips and removed the splints. Then he washed his hands.

Lindley turned away as Dr. Grayson examined Dora's leg. He couldn't bear to see her injury.

"It's good you sent for me when you did. Time is of the essence. It's critical that surgery begin immediately." He turned to Dr. Unger. "Where is your operating room?"

Dr. Unger held out his hands. "Just my office here."

Lindley spoke in a hoarse whisper. "You're not going to cut off her leg, are you?"

"Certainly not." Dr. Grayson swung a glare to Dr. Unger. "That would be barbaric. A doctor must first do everything in his power to save a limb. Her leg is good, and she is young. I'm sure she'll heal fast."

"Um—I—uh." Dr. Unger couldn't seem to speak. "I'm only a simple country doctor."

"So that gives you an excuse to be ignorant and the right to maim a small child unnecessarily?" Dr. Grayson shook his head and spoke in a condescending tone. "Do you have carbolic acid?"

"Of course."

"Bring it and iodine."

"I'm almost out of iodine."

"What kind of practice are you running here?"

"I have some on order."

Dr. Grayson took a controlled breath. "Get me some whiskey."

"Whiskey?" Lindley would not let a drunken doctor touch his daughter. He didn't care how good he was.

"Don't be ridiculous," Dr. Grayson snapped. "It's to clean my hands and the incision."

"But you washed your hands."

"I will not have my every action questioned. If so, your daughter will die before I have a chance to treat her. Now leave."

Lindley straightened his shoulders. "I'm staying with my daughter."

Dr. Grayson narrowed his eyes. "I cannot operate with you here. So either you leave, or I will." He shifted his gaze to Bridget.

She took Lindley by the arm and led him toward the door.

Lindley turned back. "You won't cut off her leg?"

The doctor's lips thinned. "I have no intention of performing an unnecessary amputation. Go!"

With a heavy heart, Lindley stepped out into the waiting room.

As Bridget was closing the door behind them, the doctor said, "Dr. Unger, you will assist me."

Lindley turned to Bridget. "He won't take her leg?"

"No. He is one of the best surgeons in the West. He has the skills to repair it. Why don't you sit and rest?"

He nodded and sat on the bench. His poor little girl.

"I'll go get you some food."

He shook his head. "I'm not hungry."

"You need to eat something. You must keep your strength up for Dora."

He stood. "Is she going to be all right?"

"Yes. I'll bring something, and you can eat what you feel like."

He nodded and crossed to the door to the other room. He wanted to be with his daughter.

Bridget touched his arm. "You can't go in there. The doctor needs to work undisturbed."

"I know." He pressed his palm to the door. "If I could just hear her breathing, I'd know she was all right."

"Sit and rest."

"I can't. I need to move." He strode back across the room. He wished he had a sledgehammer and could pulverize some limestone.

"I'll be back as soon as I can," she said as she left.

He was alone. An empty ache opened up inside him. *Lord Jesus...Jesus...Jesus.* No other words would come.

He slumped down onto the bench, put his head in his hands and cried.

Within the hour, Bridget returned, not only with food, but Cilla and Gabe, as well.

Gabe ran to him and threw his arms around his waist. "I'm sorry."

Lindley picked up his son and held him close. "It's not your fault. Everything is going to be all right." He coaxed Gabe into eating and ate a little himself. Bridget had been right; it did make him feel better. As did having Gabe, Cilla and Bridget near.

Sometime later, the door opened, and Dr. Unger emerged. "Mr. Thompson, you may go in."

Lindley crossed the room in a few quick strides. "How is she?"

"She came through fine."

Cilla and Gabe followed but the doctor held up his hand. "Only the father."

Lindley nodded to his sister and entered the room.

Dr. Grayson had a stethoscope pressed to Dora's chest.

His little girl appeared to be sleeping peacefully, her leg wrapped and splinted again. He stepped softly over to the exam table and whispered, "How is she?"

Dr. Grayson pulled the earpieces away from his head. He spoke in a normal volume. "She's too medicated to hear you. She'll be fine. Her leg should heal without trouble." He moved to the door and opened it. "Bridget."

The rush of scuffling feet and then a soft reply. Bridget and the doctor spoke in low voices, and Lindley couldn't hear what they were saying. Bridget shook her head and appeared to be upset.

Lindley crossed the room to where they were standing. "What is it?"

Dr. Grayson said to Bridget, "I did as you asked. Now go."

Lindley took controlled breaths. "If it concerns my daughter, I have a right to know."

The doctor and Bridget had their gazes locked.

Though Dr. Grayson spoke to him, his focus stayed on Bridget. "This doesn't concern you, Mr. Thompson. Go back to your daughter. Make sure she doesn't stir and fall off the table."

Lindley jerked his attention back to Dora and returned to her side. He wanted to call Bridget in, but when he looked up, she was gone.

Dr. Grayson moved to Dora's side, as well. "I've sent Dr. Unger to procure a bed and have it brought here. The child should be moved as little as possible for the next two days."

"I appreciate you coming at Miss Greene's request. I can't thank you enough."

Dr. Grayson narrowed his eyes. "Miss Greene? Bridget?"

"Yes."

The doctor squared his shoulders. "It's time you knew the truth. Her surname is not Greene. It's Grayson." He turned and marched away.

Grayson? Couldn't be. The doctor had seemed a bit possessive toward Bridget. And Bridget obeyed his orders. But what was their relationship? Was he husband or father? Men like Dr. Grayson often took a much younger wife. Lindley hoped he was only her father. If he was very fortunate, he was a much older brother or uncle.

Lindley sat at his daughter's bedside at his home.

Dr. Grayson stayed in town for two more days to make sure Dora's recovery was on track, to fashion a plaster cast on her leg and to oversee her being transported home. Once Dora was settled in her bed, he listened to her heart through his stethoscope one last time.

Dora put her tiny hand on his cheek. "Where is Miss Greene?"

He pulled away and scowled. "She's gone." He closed his medical bag and then spoke to Lindley. "She should be carried the next few days. Then crutches. No weight on that leg. That's important." He strode out of the room and went to the front door.

Lindley followed.

"Let me know your fee, and I'll pay you now."

"No need. My fee has been sufficiently paid."

"Where's Bridget?" No matter how many times Lindley had asked, the doctor wouldn't tell him anything more about Bridget or where she was. Lindley hadn't seen Bridget since just after Dora's surgery. She hadn't even said goodbye.

"She's none of your concern."

"You sent her away, didn't you?"

"Yes."

Lindley took a deep breath. "Are you her father or husband?"

"What does it matter? Either way, she belongs to me."

Belonged to him? He made it sound as if she were a slave. "It matters."

Dr. Grayson studied him a moment. "If you must know, she's my daughter. When she ran away three years ago, she was betrothed to a very wealthy man. She disgraced me and my good name. She had a responsibility to family and failed to honor her promise. She left the poor man waiting. But she's returned to where she belongs. To fulfill *all* her promises. You had best forget all about her."

Lindley stared in disbelief. Bridget was betrothed? She had gone back on her word? How could she? "But…?"

The doctor heaved a breath. "She is promised to another man."

Zachariah March, no doubt. He wished he'd never taken her to that party. He wished he could go back to the life when he was a lowly miner and she a simple schoolteacher. Back to a time when he ate supper at her table every night, as though he and Bridget and the children were a family. An empty place opened up inside him where his heart once was.

"She will marry as soon as it can be arranged. I advise you again to forget all about her. Good day." The doctor turned abruptly and left.

If only Lindley *could* forget her.

It had been a week since Dora's accident. She no longer required medicine for pain, and her leg was healing.

Lindley's heart was another matter. Bridget had been engaged the whole time. She had run out on her family. And she had let him fall in love with her when she was not free to do so. How could he ever trust her again? He let the hurt and anger fester every minute of every day.

After putting Gabe to bed, he checked on Dora. She lay asleep on her back with both arms wrapped around Bridget's fancy porcelain clock she'd left for his little girl. He freed it and set it on the bedside table, trying not to look at it or think of the woman it once belonged to. He kissed Dora's forehead. Slipping out, he pulled the door almost closed so he could hear if she woke, and returned to the parlor.

But before he could sit, his sister planted herself in front of him with her hands on her hips. "Lindley?"

"Don't, Cilla. Don't even speak her name."

"You're just going to let another man make her his wife?"

"It's probably already done. There is nothing I can do." He just wanted to forget all about her so the ache inside him would go away.

"You're not even going to fight for her?"

He had no fight left in him. "Stop. You'll only upset the children."

"Too late. Bridget's absence and your behavior already have."

Lindley cringed at the mention of her name. "Cilla, if you don't refrain from speaking of her, I'll send you back home."

She folded her arms. "Then who will look after your children?"

"I don't know!" He couldn't think. He just wanted her to stop pestering him about something he could do nothing about.

Chapter 18

Lindley wanted to return to his home in the middle of the island. A week and a half had passed since Bridget left, and he still hadn't been able to banish her from his head. If he could leave Roche Harbor, maybe he could forget about her. But he needed to remain a few days longer before Dora could travel. She had a cast and had started using crutches to get around, and she was back to her old, happy self.

He left the mining office and strode toward the house he was forced to continue living in until he could move back home. His work here was completed for the time being and all he wanted to do was go.

A stunning brunette shaded by a parasol approached him. She wore an expensive pink gown. The same color Bridget had worn to the party.

No. Stop thinking of her.

"Are you Mr. Lindley Thompson?"

"I am."

She halted in front of him. "How is Dora healing?"

Who was this woman? How did she know about Dora? "She's healing fine. Thanks to Dr. Grayson. And you are?"

"Where are my manners?" She held out a gloved hand. "I'm Mrs. Delfina March."

Lindley stared at the woman's hand a moment before

taking it and nodding over it. "Mrs. March, pleased to meet you. How do you know of my daughter?"

"Please call me Fina."

"Ma'am, we've only just met. It would be inappropriate for me to use your given name." It was more because he didn't like the advantage this woman had knowing who he was and about his daughter.

Her wide mouth pulled up at the corners. "She said you were polite."

Who had been talking about him to this woman? Certainly she hadn't come to inquire about his daughter, a child she'd never met. "What can I do for you?"

"I have news of Bridget, but if you want to hear it, you must call me Fina."

His heart beat faster at the mention of Bridget. He whispered her name. "Bridget? Is she well?" He had no right to ask. She was engaged to another, probably married, and he couldn't trust her. But at the same time, he found he couldn't resist. He needed to know how she was. "Would you care to join me in the hotel dining room for a lemonade...Fina?"

Her mouth broke into a wide smile, and she hooked her hand into the crook of his elbow. "I would love to."

There was something familiar about this woman, but he couldn't figure out what. He couldn't say that he'd ever seen her before. What was it?

Once they were seated and the lemonades served, he waited for the woman to speak. She had obviously come wanting to impart information. Not wanting to seem eager, he feigned contentment and sipped the tart drink.

She gave him a sympathetic look. "You poor dear. You look like a thirsty man in the desert, yearning for water he can see but not drink."

That could describe how he felt. "Mrs.—Fina, you sought me out. If you have something you wish to tell me, then please do. I have work to attend to." Not really, but he was hoping to hurry her along.

She took a sip and then set down her glass. "Bridget is not faring well."

He sat up straighter. "Her husband-to-be isn't mistreating her, is he?" Zachariah. He had seemed like a decent fellow. But obviously not.

"Husband-to-be? Oh, no. There is no future husband. At least, not yet. But there is no time to waste."

"Wait. Zachariah March. Then who…?"

"My husband? He said he'd met you and hoped you would make Bridget happy. Because that would make me happy."

March. It wasn't this woman who was familiar; it was her name. It had taken his brain long enough to connect the two.

She took another sip of lemonade. "But we were talking about Bridget."

"Her father told me she is betrothed." If not to Zachariah, then someone else. "That's why she left…" …*me*.

"Yes, a colleague of his who could further his career. A man old enough to be her father. That was three years ago. He has passed away. Her father is seeking out another suitable match for her. I think you should apply."

Apply? She made it sound like an employment solicitation. A tingle of joy leaped to life at the news she wasn't already married.

"She loves you. You are the only person who can pull her out of her despondency."

"She lied to me. How can I trust her? Or even believe she loves me?" She hadn't said so. But then, he had stopped her.

"After what she did for your daughter, you doubt her love?"

"She asked her father to perform surgery and then left without a word."

"Is that what you really think? She exchanged *her* life for *your* daughter's. She gave up *her* freedom and a happy future so *your* daughter would walk. She had to beg her father to do the surgery. In exchange, she agreed to return home and marry the man of his choosing. Those were his terms, not hers.

"She loves you and your children so much, she gave you all up so Dora could walk. That is the depth of her love. 'Greater love hath no man—or woman—than this, that a man lay down his life for his friends.' Indeed, I wonder if you ever truly loved her."

"I do love her—did love her. But she lied about who she was. She led me to believe she was a simple schoolteacher when she was in fact some heiress."

"I wouldn't call her an heiress, but she does stand to inherit a considerable amount of money now that she has gone home and promised to do her father's bidding. When you met her, she *was* a simple schoolteacher. She had given up the money, the lavish home, the servants, the fancy dresses and the extravagant parties to teach children. She wanted to marry you when she thought you were just a miner. You are a man of duplicitous standards."

"How so?"

"When you met her, weren't you pretending to be a poor miner when in fact you were working for management? Not only did you lie to Bridget but all the men you worked with, as well."

"That was for my job. I helped make conditions better for the miners and their families. Better homes to live in and safer conditions on the job. The men would not have trusted me if they'd known who I was."

"But still it was deception, was it not? The very thing you're criticizing her for. How is she to trust you?"

He didn't want to admit that Fina was right. He'd behaved abominably. "But what am I to do?"

Fina smiled and clasped her hands together. "I knew you had to be a reasonable man. Go to Anacortes, declare your love for her and steal her away."

That sounded like something his older sister would tell him to do. If it were only that easy. "What about her father? He told me to forget about her."

She waved a dismissive hand in the air between them. "Don't let him stand in the way of your love. She is miserable without you."

And he without her. "She's truly not married? Or betrothed?"

She shook her head.

Thinking she was married had helped him to not go running after her. He'd fueled his anger by picturing her in the arms of another man…married. "I need to get my children settled with my parents or one of my sisters first."

"Take them with you."

"But Dora…?

"When can she travel?"

"She's doing well, but I'd like to wait a few more days."

Fina clapped her hands in much the same way Dora did when she was excited. "Then it's all settled. Early next week, you and your delightful children will come to Anacortes. You will stay with Zachariah and me. We won't tell her you're coming. We'll surprise her." She touched her gloved index finger to her lips.

"I'll make arrangements for my sister to go back home."

"Nonsense. Bring her along. So you *will* come?"

"Yes."

"I won't let her father marry her off before you arrive. I will lay down my life before I will let that happen."

Fina and his sister Rachel would get along well. Both were hopeless romantics, and now they were rubbing off on him. He was turning into a romantic himself. He guessed that was what true love did to a person.

Chapter 19

The following Monday, Lindley stood with sweaty palms outside the Grayson mansion. He never would have guessed that Bridget came from this kind of money. If she had stayed here, she never would have had to teach or do work of any kind. Yet, according to Fina, she had been willing to marry him when he was a mere miner. A very hard life.

How could he have not trusted in her love? She hadn't said she loved him in words. But he could see now that her actions yelled it loud and clear. Her sacrifice for his daughter was a debt he could never repay.

He wiped his hands on his trousers and lifted the door knocker once. It sounded with a thud that he could almost hear echo inside.

How could he have thought that arranged marriages were all right? Some perhaps, if both people were willing, but the thought of Bridget being forced to marry a man she didn't want to was—as she had said—archaic and barbaric.

He hoped her father hadn't pressed for a wedding. Fina said she would do what she could to prevent Bridget from getting married before he could plead his case. But when he'd arrived in town, Fina had said that Dr. Grayson refused to let her visit Bridget anymore. And Bridget wasn't allowed to go out until she was married off. She was essentially a prisoner in her own home.

The thick oak door opened slowly. He expected it to creak or give a great bellowing moan. But it did neither. As silent as a whisper.

A white-haired man in a black suit, crisp white shirt and black bow tie stood on the other side of the threshold. "Good day, sir. May I help you?"

"I would like to see Bridget Gree—Grayson."

"May I ask who is calling?"

"Lindley Thompson."

The man stepped aside. "Right this way."

As Lindley entered, the marble entry floor seemed to echo even his breathing. A curving staircase of mahogany ascended to the upper floor. At least two of the mining-company shanties could fit in this entry. The vastness and splendor of the house dwarfed his self-confidence. He felt like an errant child trespassing where he shouldn't. He could almost hear his own heartbeat.

The man shut the front door and slid open a pocket door to the right. "Please wait in here."

Lindley found himself in a large room lined with bookshelves from floor to ceiling without space for a single volume more. He heard the door slide quietly closed behind him.

No wonder Bridget made such a good teacher. She'd had all these books to read. Even if she read only a small portion of them, her knowledge would be vast.

He tilted his head and read the titles on the spines. Shelves and shelves of medical books. He stepped across the room to see what other subjects were there and stopped at a volume on mining. He pulled it out. Interesting. What was a doctor doing with a book on mining? He scanned other titles and noted that there were volumes on various topics.

"What are you doing here?" A gruff voice snapped behind him.

Lindley juggled the book between his hands but ultimately lost control, and it careened to the carpeted floor with a dull thud. "I'm sorry." He hurriedly retrieved it and shoved it back onto the shelf. Then he turned to see Dr. Grayson glaring at him.

"I forbid you to see Bridget. You may leave now. Orvin will show you out." The doctor turned to retreat.

"Wait."

Dr. Grayson swung back around, glaring.

In that moment, Lindley knew why he was really here and swallowed hard. "I wish to speak with *you*."

"About my daughter, no doubt."

Yes. But he sensed it would be more. "I would like to tell you about your daughter. Shall we sit?"

Lindley strolled back to Fina and Zachariah's home. He couldn't believe he'd spent several hours the past three days talking to Bridget's father. And not once had he asked to see Bridget. He wanted to see her, hoped the doctor would offer, but never asked. Though each conversation started out about Bridget, it always turned to God.

The poor doctor didn't know the Lord.

Lindley couldn't imagine going through life's trials without the solid foundation his faith brought him. How could he have gotten through Dora's injury, his wife's dying or hanging on for dear life over a cliff at age twelve? It was his night on the cliff that had made God real to him.

Perhaps Dr. Grayson needed his own cliff experience to see his need for the Lord.

As Lindley climbed the steps of the wide porch of the March mansion, the door opened.

The butler dipped his head. "Good afternoon, sir. Welcome back."

Lindley stepped inside. He was not used to people waiting on him. But this was the station Bridget came from. Money, servants and grandeur. Maybe she had been relieved to be done with him. She hadn't said she loved him. But he hoped she did.

Cilla rushed up to him. "Did you talk to her today?"

He shook his head. "It wasn't the right time to ask."

"Not the right time? Tomorrow is the last day. We leave the following day."

"I know. I know." He handed his hat to the butler. "Thank you."

Cilla didn't let up. "Is her father any closer to letting you see her?"

"It's hard to say. There are times when I'm telling him about God and Jesus that he seems to be really listening and interested. Then it's like a massive door slams shut between us. He told me not to come back."

"And what did you say?"

"That I'd see him tomorrow."

"What if he's not there?" Cilla asked.

"He'll be there." He had to be.

"How do you know?"

"Fear."

Cilla squinted her face.

"He would be afraid that I'd show up and see Bridget at the house. Or if she wasn't there, that one of his household staff would have pity on me and tell me where she is."

"Why don't you go to the house when he's not there and see her?"

He shook his head. "It wouldn't be right to go around him. I need his blessing. He needs to see me as honorable."

Cilla huffed. "Well, at this rate, dear brother, you'll be an old man before you see her again."

"Tomorrow I'm going to ask to see her."

"And if he refuses?"

"I can't think that way." He would see her, one way or another. He had to.

As Bridget sat on a bench in the rear garden, her father strode out of the house and approached her. "Bridget, why must you wear that dreadful black dress every day?"

"I'm in mourning." Her father had forbidden her to leave the house or grounds. He'd even put an end to all her visitors. Especially Fina.

"I don't find that humorous. No one has died."

She hadn't meant it as humorous. "My freedom has. It was murdered."

He scowled.

Now his expression was humorous. She stood to leave.

"Eat supper with me."

She gritted her teeth and said, "Our agreement didn't include suppers or polite conversation. Only a perfect son-in-law for you." She strolled toward the house.

"Don't walk away from me."

There was a time, not so long ago, she wouldn't have dared to defy that order. Now it only caused the slightest hesitation in her step.

He called after her. "Why are this man and his children so important to you?"

That made her stop, but she didn't turn around right away. When she did, she was slow and deliberate. "I love him and love his children. Something you don't understand."

"Eat supper with me and plead your case."

Supplication from her father? Doubtful. More likely manipulation to get what he wanted.

"That would be a waste of my time and yours." She strode away knowing that no amount of pleading or crying on her part would change his mind.

As the afternoon pushed toward supper, an annoying prompting to eat with her father kept badgering Bridget. She tried to ignore it. But couldn't. She didn't want to sup with the man forcing her into marriage. Wouldn't. She could be as stubborn as him.

But the Lord poked and prodded her until she was spiritually black-and-blue. So when the supper hour arrived, she found herself descending the staircase. She took a deep breath before braving the threshold into the dining room.

Her father sat at the far end of the long table with several folders spread out around his plate. He didn't notice her.

The cook's assistant standing at Father's elbow cleared her throat. "Sir."

He looked up, and the servant made a pointed look at Bridget.

Her father stood. "Come sit." He turned to the woman and indicated the seat adjacent to him. "Bring another place setting."

The woman scurried out.

Bridget was tempted to seat herself at the far opposite end of the table but sat where she was expected to. Why had she come?

He sat again. "I sent Pinkerton detectives all over the country looking for you."

Not surprising.

"I feared the worst."

"Well, as you can see, I'm hale and hearty."

He scowled at her retort. "I never imagined you would go to the islands. You hate traveling by boat."

That was why she had chosen the islands. She knew it would be the last place he would look. "Still do."

He was silent for a few moments before he spoke again. "So you have come to convince me to change my mind. I'm interested in what arguments you will use."

"No, I haven't. If I learned one thing living under your roof, it is that once you have made a decision, there is no changing your mind. Even if you are wrong."

The servant set a plate, silverware, goblet and all the other unnecessary utensils around her plate. What a waste.

"Thank you, Millicent."

The woman stared at her a moment. The staff wasn't used to anyone thanking them for the duties they performed daily. Her father certainly never had.

She curtsied and backed away.

Her father waited until the servants had dished up food onto her plate and left before he spoke. "So if you didn't come to petition for your freedom, why are you here?"

He would love for her to beg, probably prefer it if she got down on her knees. "I don't know. I guess I feel sorry for you." That surprised her. When had she started feeling sorry for him? And for what? He had everything.

He narrowed his eyes. Evidently not approving of her reason.

She took a bite of roast lamb. She hadn't eaten so elaborately in years. Her palate didn't much care for it, but she forced the meat down her throat. Or maybe it was the company that disagreed with her. "Have you chosen… someone?" She couldn't bring herself to say "a husband."

"I have a few men in mind." He took a drink of his wine, studying her over the rim of the glass. Looking for a reaction, no doubt.

She would give him none and took a bite of asparagus.

He set his glass down. "So this Mr. Thompson? He's like you? Pious?"

This she did react to. By staring. Her father never spoke

of religion and forbade anyone in his presence to speak of it. "Yes...he believes in God."

"Is this why you care for him?"

"I guess it's part of it because loving God makes him the man he is."

"No one made me the man I am. I have done everything on my own. This God is nothing more than a crutch for weak men." He took a bite of lamb.

So her father had brought up the subject so he could criticize God. And criticize her for believing in Him.

He swallowed. "You apparently had the life you wanted and could have married this man. Why did you contact me?"

"A little girl's life was at stake."

"She would have lived."

"But Dr. Unger wanted to amputate her leg."

"She would have learned to get around with an artificial one."

She couldn't believe he could be so indifferent.

"So why me, and not some other doctor?"

"The only doctors I know are your colleagues, and they would have run to you and told you where I was. You are the best. Why settle for second best when you would find out anyway? And I had no guarantee any of them would have come posthaste."

"Still, you could have had everything you wanted in exchange for her leg. A rather small price to pay. So why did you choose her over yourself?"

Of course her father couldn't understand. "It was the right thing to do. How could I have lived out my life knowing I cost a little girl her leg? Why should Dora pay the price for my freedom?"

"None of them would have known. They would have accepted it as part of life."

"I would have known." Her father was unbelievable. She set her napkin on the table. "I've lost my appetite."

"Running away because you don't like the way a conversation is going?" There was that soft, docile tone that challenged.

Would she be baited? "Why bother with me, Father? You got what you wanted. Once you marry me off, you'll be done with me." She stood.

When she was halfway to the doorway, he spoke. "I am a highly intelligent man. There isn't anything I can't learn, comprehend or do. But this is one thing I can't understand, sacrificing oneself for another."

Bridget froze at the threshold. Did her father truly desire to understand? Or was he manipulating her? Saying the words he was sure would get her to stay.

If there was even the slightest chance he was genuinely interested, she had to tell him about the love of God.

She returned to her seat.

Chapter 20

Lindley sat in the Marches' parlor with his children, sister and Fina. Cilla and Fina were devising plans to ensure he would get to talk to Bridget that day. He doubted any of them would work. They didn't know Dr. Grayson the way he did. They didn't understand how hard-hearted and unyielding the man was.

The door knocker thudded. A few moments later, the butler entered the parlor. "Mr. Thompson, a gentleman to see you."

Lindley stared disbelievingly at Dr. Grayson standing beside the butler.

The doctor surveyed the roomful of people. "Mr. Thompson, I have business to discuss with you."

Lindley stood. On one hand, sitting was disrespectful to his visitor; on the other, the standing man exerted primacy over the sitting. Lindley had no desire to insult Bridget's father or allow him to dominate any discussion they might have. "What business?" He hoped it would be about Bridget but she wasn't business. She was personal. At least to Lindley.

Dr. Grayson scowled. "In private."

Fina spoke from where she sat on the settee with Cilla. "Lindley, would you like the rest of us to leave?"

He knew he should say yes. "You don't have to."

Fina turned a triumphant grin on Bridget's father. "State your business."

Dora crutched over to Dr. Grayson, stood two inches in front of him and tilted her head back.

Dr. Grayson's eyebrows twitched. "I—uh— What does this child want?"

Lindley struggled not to smile. For all the doctor's self-assurance, unshakable beliefs and inflexibility, little Dora had rattled him. "Ask her."

The doctor scowled and looked down.

"You fixed my leg," Dora said.

"Yes. Now run along."

Dora remained in place. "Are you Miss Greene's papa?"

He took a controlled breath in and let it out. "I am."

"Then I love you." Dora let her crutches fall to the floor and gripped the older man around the legs.

Dr. Grayson stiffened. "Please control your child."

Lindley rather liked seeing the haughty doctor uncomfortable. But before he did or said something to hurt Dora, Lindley stepped across the room and picked up his daughter. "She doesn't bite." Well, there was that time when she was two and bit Gabe, but he wouldn't mention that.

The doctor's face pulled back as though he'd eaten something rancid. "I put that cast on her leg."

Why did that bother him? He *was* the one who had done it.

"Yes."

Dora swung her injured leg. "It makes my other leg stronger."

Dr. Grayson scowled. "That backwoods, incompetent doctor. He was supposed to take that off and remove the sutures." He reached into his inside coat pocket and handed Lindley a card. "Meet me at my office in thirty minutes." He turned abruptly and left.

Lindley stared after him.

"That was rude," Fina said.

Cilla added, "He never stated his business."

Apparently, medicine eclipsed everything else for the proud doctor.

An hour later, Lindley sat next to Dora in the doctor's office. Dr. Grayson had shown Dora a jar of peppermint candies and told her if she didn't cause a fuss, she could have one. He had let Dora poke his hand with the blunt-nosed scissors he'd use to cut away her cast so she could see they wouldn't hurt her. He was far better with patients than people outside his office.

Dora pointed to her leg. "Are those my soochies?"

"Sutures," the doctor corrected. "Yes. You must keep your leg very still. The bone inside is still fragile. You will feel a little tug as I pull out the sutures. Can you count them?"

Dora nodded.

One by one, the threads were clipped and removed. Dora scrunched up her face as the first few were removed but didn't cry or fuss. "Eleven," she declared when the last one was gone. She had a red scar down the side of her calf as well as yellowish bruises.

Lindley held his breath while Dr. Grayson probed where the break was.

Dora sucked in air between clenched teeth, and her head shook, but she didn't move the rest of her body or fuss. Once a new cast was on her leg and the doctor had told her to sit very still until it dried, she crooked her finger and her whole arm at him.

He stepped closer. "What?"

She continued to curl her finger. "Closer."

He leaned in.

Dora tossed her arms around his neck and whispered in his ear, "I love you." At a volume that anyone could hear.

Lindley smiled at her loud whisper, her gregarious nature and her big heart.

Were those tears in Dr. Grayson's eyes?

The man's arms moved slowly…but eventually made their way around Dora in a hug.

Bridget sat in the window seat in her room, gazing out at the back garden in full summer's bloom. She ignored the soft knock on her door just as the servants ignored her pleas for them to go away and leave her alone. But they had their orders.

The door opened, and Petunia, her lady's maid, stepped inside and gave a quick curtsy. "Miss?"

She turned to the young woman, wanting to tell the servant to go, but it wasn't her fault. Her father had sent her, no doubt.

"Your father wishes to speak with you."

She shifted her focus back out the window. "Tell him I'm not feeling up to it." She would never be up to speaking with him again.

His deep voice said, "You seem quite healthy to me."

Bridget blinked thrice before swinging her gaze to her father. She couldn't remember him *ever* entering her room. People came to the great Dr. Grayson; he did not stoop to going to them. This was strange indeed.

"Well, I'm feeling quite peaked." She wanted to say that with all his education, a seasoned doctor should be able to see that for himself. But that would be impudent. And he could figure out her meaning.

"That dress is ghastly." He commented every day on the inappropriateness of her dress.

She didn't care. Her simple black frock had few adornments. The ugliest gown in her wardrobe. "I like it. It suits me."

"It won't do to receive your future husband."

Her insides tightened. So he had finally chosen. She wanted to argue and plead with him but knew it would do no good. Tears stung her eyes. She blinked them away.

This was exactly what she would wear to greet her intended. Maybe the man would change his mind when he saw her. She rose from the sill as regal as a queen heading off to her execution.

"Petunia." Her father flicked his wrist. "Find something suitable in her dressing room. Something with a little color to it."

The servant darted into the adjoining room.

"Don't bother, Father. I'll wear what I have on."

He lowered his voice but not to the usual commanding tone. Still, it left little room for arguing. "You will change your gown if I have to dress you myself."

He would never do that, but he might get the maids to team up and wrangle her out of her present attire. He was acting strange. She couldn't put her finger on it, but there was something unusual about his behavior. Even the way he stood.

Bridget was still locked in a visual conflict with the man who sired her when Petunia returned with her arms loaded. Bridget supposed this was a battle her father would ultimately win.

She shifted her gaze to the three gowns Petunia laid out on her bed. One mint green, another in bright blue and the third in the palest of pinks. All exquisitely pleasing, gorgeous, beautiful.

If she must change, she would wear the beige one hanging in the back of her closet. The second-ugliest dress she owned, with frayed cuffs and collar. She headed for her dressing-room door.

"One of these, Bridget. The green one makes your eyes come alive. I expect to see you downstairs in ten minutes in one of those gowns." He pointed toward her bed and then strode out of the room.

She wanted to scream, stamp her feet and throw something breakable at the closed door. How strange for him to suggest a dress choice.

"Miss? The green would look lovely. You would steal his heart with one look for sure."

That was the last thing she wanted. She would definitely *not* wear the green one. If she made herself as undesirable as possible, maybe her father's choice would decline the betrothal. She tamped down her anger and shifted her gaze to the offensive dresses. Each one beautiful and among her favorites at one time. Petunia had obeyed her master's orders well in these choices.

The blue was bold and commanding. But the pink one, being so pale, would likely wash out her complexion and make her look sickly. The thought of being forced to marry did nauseate her. So the question was, did she want to be commanding or appear pallid?

A few minutes later, she exited her bedroom to find her father in the hallway. Had he waited to make sure she indeed had followed his orders? He gave a nod of approval. His behavior was getting stranger and stranger.

"Miss Greene!" Dora hobbled over on stubby crutches.

Bridget instinctively scooped up the little girl. The crutches fell to the carpeted floor. She drank in the scent of the child's innocence. This meant Lindley was here.

Was her father telling her he had chosen Lindley? Or was this some new cruel trick to make her face her betrothed in Lindley's presence?

He picked up the crutches and motioned toward the staircase for her to go first. "The blue suits you."

She had chosen commanding over ill. Strength over weakness. She would not cower before her fate. She lifted her chin and headed toward her future, whatever that might be. Excitement and hope warred with dread.

From behind her, he said, "I understand."

Understand what? Her trepidation? She doubted that.

Uncharacteristically, Dora remained silent and laid her head on Bridget's shoulder, content to be in her arms.

Each step she took a little faster. She stopped at the threshold to the parlor.

Fina and Cilla smiled up at her from the settee with Gabe wedged between them.

Lindley stood near the hearth, looking as handsome as ever.

Bridget surveyed the room. No one else was present. She glanced at her father.

"I finally understand sacrifice. Yours and God's." He took Dora from her arms.

"Oh, Father. Really?"

He nodded.

That was what was behind the strangeness and his atypical behavior. He'd been changed. There was a softness to his gaze. A tenderness that had never been there before.

He tilted his head toward the room. "He's waiting."

She turned back to find Lindley standing right in front of her. He took her hand and lowered to one knee, holding out a diamond ring. "Will you marry me?"

Simple and to the point. That was one of the things she loved about him. No extra words to confuse things. No false vibrato. No fancy musings. "Yes. Very much yes."

He bolted to his feet and kissed her.

She wanted to linger in his embrace, but Gabe said, "Eeeeew."

Everyone in the room laughed, including Bridget and Lindley.

Lindley said, "When can we marry?"

"Anytime you want to."

He raised his eyebrows. "Today."

"What about your parents?"

Before Lindley could answer, Cilla jumped up. "They won't mind. They will be happy for him."

Then Lindley said, "How much time do you need to plan the wedding?"

"I don't need anything elaborate. Just you and me and a preacher." She didn't want to give her father time to change his mind.

Surprisingly, her father said, "Then today it is. Orvin, send for a clergyman."

He really had changed. Bridget couldn't believe this amazing transformation. She had prayed for this but never thought it would really happen.

Her father tilted his head. "You're staring. It's very unladylike."

"What brought about this change?"

"I saw the difference in you. Then my son-in-law-to-be was quite persistent." He shifted his focus to Dora still in his arms. "And this little one has a heart full of love. I found I lost all desire to resist."

Dora kissed him on the cheek.

Sweet little Dora.

An hour later, the minister said, "I now pronounce you husband and wife. You may kiss your bride."

Lindley wasted no time.

A giddiness tingled all over her at the touch of his lips on hers.

He kissed her far longer than was appropriate in the midst of others, especially her father and the children. But she didn't care.

She was Mrs. Lindley Thompson, just who she was meant to be. A daughter held in respect. A wife cherished with love. A mother blessed by two adorable children and the possibility of more.

* * * * *